DENSITY

BRETT SAMPSON

Density

ISBN 979-87076472-2-2

First Printing 2021

To my mom. My number one fan. June Sloan.

Chapter 1

Jack's alarm pierced the black night like a high-pitched bullfrog croaking over and over at regular intervals. His eyes shot open, and then slowly closed again. He reached and found the off button on his bedside clock. Silence, bullfrog. The clock read 6:11. An odd time to set your alarm clock, but to Jack 6:10 was too early to get up, and he really didn't want to set the number to 6:12. So, the wake-up time was obvious.

It was still dark in Jack's room at 6:11 on the November Texas morning. He swung his long legs over the edge of his tousled up bed. With his feet hanging in the air, Jack ran his right hand through his hair trying to bring his mind out of the fog of sleep. Finally he rubbed his eyes, and stood up on the carpet runner that ran along the edge of his bed. Jack was a strapping young man. Twenty three years old. Six feet two inches tall. A thick head of dark hair had a mind of it's own from a night of fighting with his pillow. He had broad muscular shoulders on top of a lean muscular frame. Slowly moving into the already stirring kitchen Jack Strong stopped at the coffee pot. Barefoot, in blue boxer shorts, and a ratty t-shirt. Yawning with his eyes closed, Jack knew exactly where to stand to open the cupboard and get his favorite cup.

As he often did, Jack was running through in his mind a kind of a task list of what he needed to accomplish that day. Afterall, though he was a young man, Jack had the mantle and responsibility of a much older man. Upon the death of his father four years ago, Jack took over the metal shop his father ran, and more importantly he took over the responsibility of providing for his little brother Jimmy, and his mom. Many his age would try to shirk the heavy burden, but not Jack. He had played football in high school, with some acclaim, and he had received offers to play football for three colleges. He occasionally wonders what life would have been like if his dad hadn't died, and he had gone to college and played football. But, alas it was just not to be, as Jack reminded himself often. There was still a slice of bitterness he felt from time to time about a lost opportunity to live the life he chose for himself, but when it came to his family there was really no other choice to be made. He did the right thing. The thing a grown man would do. He decided to make the best of it, and he'd been trying to do that every day since he made the decision.

"Happy birthday!." said Jack's mom, with as much excitement she could muster for six A.M., her wiry grey hair fell just past her shoulders. June Strong had a well worn green robe on with a faded spot covering most of the left forearm. This time of morning she walked with a slight limp from knee surgery that was now six months ago. It just took her knees a little longer to wake up, as she was fond of telling Jack with a smile.

"What? Oh yeah?" Jack asked while rubbing his eyes.

"Just seems like Tuesday to me."

"My boy is twenty three years old today. I made your favorite breakfast this morning." said June with a smile in her voice.

"Chocolate cake?" said Jack, with just a note of sarcasm.

"Yes, Chocolate cake. No! Breakfast, silly"

"I think I had chocolate cake for breakfast once. Last week I think."

"Shut up. Your arm feeling better?"

Jack sat his steaming cup of coffee down on the table. He straightened his right arm out, and moved his hand up and down in a karate chop motion. A week ago Jack had injured his arm while moving a metal press break in his shop with a few of his employees.

"Yeah, I don't even feel it anymore," said Jack.

"I worry about you at that shop. Every day you have a new bump or scratch or ache or pain. I didn't want that life for you," she said as she put a plate in front of Jack. Scrambled eggs and toast.

"Let's not go down that road again, Mom." said Jack, taking a bite out of his toast. "College just wasn't in the cards for me, besides I like the shop." Jack knew his mom. She felt perpetual guilt for what happened with Jack taking over the shop and she was a bit of a drama queen as they say, so Jack knew not to pour any gas on potential fires. Besides, it was too early to be getting into any animated conversations.

"You may like it, but you are there because you didn't think you had a choice, and that's what I'm talking about."

"Most people in college are just there to figure out what they really want to do anyway and, burning through money all the while. Then after four or five years they get a degree and come back to town and get a job at the dollar store like your friend's boy. Like Martin," said Jack, while shoveling the next bite of eggs he was about to put in his mouth.

"Seriously. I like everything about the shop. Besides, who would look after you and Jimmy?"

June sat her coffee cup down on the table with a clunk. "We've been over this. Don't you bring that up to me again. Jimmy and I would be just fine."

"I'm just saying..." said Jack.

"Enough. I feel bad enough about it. Go to school if you want. We'll be fine," said June, choking up ever so slightly.

"Good lord Mom. You get so emotional. Relax. Everything is fine."

Jack sat silently, using his fork to herd up his eggs in a bite size mound.

"Jimmy is supposed to go to school early this morning for tutoring with that teacher," said June as she sat down at the table opposite Jack. She took a baby sip of her coffee before continuing. "Would you mind dropping him off on your way into work?"

"Sure. Is it math again?" Jack asked.

"Yes, teacher said he needs extra tutoring," said June as she exhaled deeply.

"Is Karen back in town from school yet?" June raised her right eyebrow a little as she inquired.

Karen Faulkner was Jack's girlfriend throughout their senior year in high school. Karen received a Tennis scholarship to the University of Missouri. She was a senior there now. Jack got a little antsy when his mom, or anyone for that matter brought up Karen. Because Jack still cared about her. He knew when Karen went off to college, and he stayed in town to work at the shop that their lives would take different paths. He told himself to let her go, because she would no doubt find some other love interest at a university as huge as Missouri. But, telling yourself to let her go, and letting her go are two different things, and Jack could never find it in himself to fully let her go. Besides, she still texted Jack. Not as often as she used to, but still *that's gotta mean something,* Jack thought.

"Not sure when she gets back," said Jack with a mouthful of eggs, avoiding eye contact with his mom.

June held her stare with a little curled smile.

"I think she gets back today," Jack admitted.

"She texted you?"

"Yes, yesterday," said Jack.

"Well for pete's sake! Why didn't you just say that?" his mom asked.

"...because, I didn't really want to talk about it, and it was easier to just say I'm not sure. Now that I think about it, it would have been just as easy to say today, but anyway... I don't want to talk about it. We aren't even together anymore."

Jack wiped his mouth, got up and put his empty plate in the sink.

"Oh, by the way you got another one of those letters from the government wanting you to get a blood test." June pointed at a letter on top of a cream colored credenza a few feet away.

"Isn't that the fifth letter they've sent you so far?" she asked.

"I told you, Mom. I'm just not going to do it."

Jack gave the letter a once over. Then he wadded it up and put it in the trash under the sink.

"The Watson Act. It's bullcrap! Every young man in this country has to have his blood tested when he turns twenty one. It's like the world was going along and then it just took a left turn into crazy. I'm not going to give the government my blood. I'm just not going to do it!"

"They have been sending these letters for two years. Something bad is going to happen if you don't go. I just know it," said June while drying her hands on a dishtowel.

"So you're going to be the Rosa Parks of the Watson Act?"

Jack looked up at his mom. "Obscure reference for my age group, but ...yeah, I guess I am. Screw them."

Jack had a stubborn streak. Which always struck Jack as strange, because neither his mom or dad was like that. They were both very easy going. It just didn't compute with Jack how the government could insist every twenty one year old young man in the United States had to give their blood. And, why? It didn't make sense to him, and he made up his mind he wasn't going to participate.

"Let me get dressed," said Jack as he walked into his bedroom. "I gotta get out of here. Is Jimmy ready?" he shouted.

"Two minutes," his mom shouted back.

Chapter 2

Jack's dad started Strong Metal Works in La Marque in nineteen ninety one. The official description for the shop was a metal fabricating shop. Basically, that involved cutting, bending, and welding metal to take different forms and functions. Since they are in such close proximity to the oil and gas industry, a lot of what they did serviced the many refineries within a fifty mile radius of La Marque. Jack took naturally to the shop, because he always had an affinity for bending, and shaping metal. He started welding in the shop around eight or nine years old. About a week and a half ago, Jack, along with his head salesman, Jim, sold the shop's biggest job to date, a three hundred unit box job to British Petroleum. These were small to medium sized stainless steel boxes that housed solenoid actuators to control fluid flow in the refinery. Jack was still on cloud nine about it. It meant pretty good money for the shop, and was going to allow him to have a healthy cash reserve. Jack always stressed about not being able to pay his employees one day, so this cash infusion made him happy.

Along with his mom, and his younger brother, Jack and his family all lived on a small farm north of town. Not an active farm. No crops. Back when his dad was alive they used to run a momma cow - baby cow operation. ...just for some extra cash. Now Jack and his mom just keep a few cows and an old bull named Blue. The sun was cresting over the horizon as Jack drove Jimmy to school in his white 2008 Ford F-150. Jimmy had his backpack resting against his legs on the floorboard. He was tall for a nine year old boy. Had sandy blond hair and freckles on his face.

"Can I tell you a secret Jimbo?" Jack said, glancing over at Jimmy.

"What?"

"I was never that great in math either."

"Really?" Jimmy smiled. "I don't like my teacher. Mrs. Cates. Fat..."

"Hey, Hey, Hey," interrupted Jack. "There's always going to be a teacher you won't like. You still have to find a way to pass the class." Jack reached over and messed up Jimmy's hair.

"Even if you don't like her, give her respect, and do what she tells you to do. Then you'll be fine."

"Hey, you know what?" asked Jimmy.

"What?" said Jack, attempting to match Jimmy's excitement level. "This morning I looked out in Blue's pen, and there was a coyote in there with him."

"A coyote? ...Really?" said Jack, surprised.

"Yeah, but it was weird. Blue wasn't scared at all. He looked at him for a minute, and then went back to eating."

"That's because old Blue is a big strong bull. He knows that coyote can't do anything to hurt him. He would swat that coyote away like it was a fly if it tried anything."

"I guess the coyote knew it too, because he didn't try anything. He just sniffed around and walked away."

Jimmy looked down at the superman action figure in his hand. "Jack, do you think it's possible Superman could ever be real?"

"No, buddy, I don't," Jack said.

"What about mutants like you see in the movies... like Wolverine? You think they could be real?"

"No, Jimmy. All that stuff is just made up. It's fiction. It would be cool if some of them were real, but it's just not possible. We live in the real world."

"But, what if the world needs a superhero to protect people when no one else can?" Jimmy said.

"Mankind has managed to survive without a superhero for this long. I think we'll be alright." Jack looked over at Jimmy, who was toying with his action figure. Jack could tell Jimmy was disappointed in his answer.

"Who knows, a superhero may come along one day. One that would help people. That would be pretty cool I guess, huh?" Jack said as he pulled into the drive that runs up to the front door of the school. The gravel crackled under his truck tires as he stopped at the front door.

He looked at Jimmy, who looked up at him and nodded with a little smile.

"Love you, bud," said Jack looking at his younger brother. "Have a good day."

"Love you too." Jimmy slung his backpack over his shoulder and shut the door on the truck. He walked towards the front door of the school looking down at the ground in front of his feet along the way.

"God I love that kid," said Jack softly to himself as he pulled away.

After making sure Jimmy got safely into the school, Jack pulled out and got on the main road headed to his shop. He knew this route well, and could drive it in his sleep. Same route he took when Jimmy's school was in session. Jack smiled to himself as he halfways wondered if his truck could make the trip by itself. The sun was up, but it wasn't all the way up yet. It stayed dark pretty late in the mornings in November. About two blocks before he was to make a turn towards his shop, Jack decided to stop at a 7-Eleven to get a cup of coffee. He pulled his truck into a space on the side of the building and immediately saw something that disturbed him.

There was a man. Looked to be in his early thirties. He stood about two feet from the exterior of the 7-Eleven, facing the wall. He was talking to himself. The thing that perplexed Jack was this guy didn't look like he should be talking to a wall outside 7-Eleven. He was well kept, and wore a suit. His hair was impeccably combed into a short side part. Looked like he had just shaved that morning.

Jack got out of his truck and walked to within about three feet of the guy.

"You okay there buddy?" Jack asked with some trepidation.

No reaction from the man. The guy had a wide eyed glassy stare about him. Wasn't blinking. Just staring at the wall. Jack stood there a moment to listen to what he was saying to himself.

"There's something wrong with this one. I can't get him to move. I can see he's looking at a wall, but no motor movement. What? Okay, I'm going to release him. I'll mark him so we can retag him."

Then the man in the suit blinked a few times and took a few stumbling steps back from the wall. Jack put his hands on his shoulders to steady him.

"You okay man?" Jack asked, trying to tone down the concern he had for the man.

"Ummm. Yeah. I think so. I was just getting a cup of coffee, and then I think I blacked out for a minute," the man in the suit said.

Then the man nodded at Jack as if to say "thank you for your help" and made his way into the store. Jack didn't mention to the guy what he was talking about when he was staring at the wall. *What was that all about,* Jack wondered. It was as if he was hearing a conversation between two people, but their voices were coming out of the man's mouth. *There had to be psychological issues with the man,* Jack thought. No other explanation. Weird, and unsettling because there seemed to be more to it than just someone talking a bunch of crazy gibberish. There was a coherent conversation. And, when they said they would release him, that's when he came out of it. Jack just had a strange feeling about the whole episode. Like it meant more than it appeared to be.

Chapter 3

Jack arrived at his shop at 6:52 am after dropping Jimmy off at school. His shop, located in an older industrial park off South Post Oak Boulevard, wasn't in the best part of town. It was a little run down, with a definite element of crime nearby, as it backed up to a neighborhood known to have a drug problem. Jack never liked it; even when he was a little kid, he never liked it. Thought the whole area was dirty, and smelled like shit most of the time, but like anything that you look at every day you end up getting used to it, and eventually you didn't even notice it anymore.

There were eleven rectangular shaped metal buildings side to side to side all the way down the block. Jack's shop was the third building down. The front of the building was beige brick about halfway up the wall, and faded red metal corrugated siding made up the rest of the exterior walls. The same red metal siding was used to construct the sides and back of the building all the way down. A large bay door was cut into each side of the building about two thirds of the way down from the front of the building.

The shop was about half as long as a football field. In the front of the building was a very small reception area. Four offices, and a small room with a table that could loosely be called a conference room. Just outside the offices was a small sink area and a refrigerator. There was also a table with six chairs where people could sit and drink coffee, or eat lunch. Beyond that was a shop designed to bend and cut metal. This consisted of six workstations for employees, two press breaks, a welding room, a sand blaster, and a portion of the space was devoted to storage of metal sheeting, expanded metal, and tubing.

Jack turned on the lights, entered his office, first door on the left. He tossed the keys to his truck on the table. Then he walked with a purpose out into the shop.

"Jack, is that you back there?" asked a tall middle-aged Black man in grey work pants and a uniformed dirty grey work shirt. The frayed patch on the shirt said *Lou Farma, Strong Metal Works.*

Jack was kneeling behind a motorcycle in the very back of the shop. If a motorcycle could have muscles, this one would be Arnold Schwarzenegger in his prime. It was beefy. Thick heavy gauge frame. Overwide wheels and tires.

"Morning, Lou. Doin' all right?" said Jack.

"Good. Good," said Lou as he inspected Jack's bike as Jack was still crouched behind it working.

"In early this morning Lou?" inquired Jack without looking up from his bike.

"No, sir. It's ten minutes till eight," said Lou, pointing at the big clock on the wall.

Jack looked up at the clock behind where Lou was standing.

"I'll be damned. Time flies I guess..." said Jack, wiping his hands on an already dirty rag next to his tool box.

"Man, are you ever going to be done with this tank of a bike?" Lou asked.

"If you mean when will it drive, I could drive it now. But, that doesn't mean I'm done working on it." Jack looked up at Lou and gave him a little smile.

"You know what the boy's been callin' it? Megatron," said Lou, laughing.

"Megatron? Like the movie you mean?" asked Jack. "Yeah, I guess it is a bit of a beast isn't it?"

11

"Why did you make the frame so bulky? So heavy?" inquired Lou, as he placed his hand on the thick rolled steel bar behind the seat.

Jack looked up and hesitated for a second. "I'm not sure really. I guess if I had to say, I'm just compelled to do it. Kinda weird, really. Plus it looks cool."

"That it does," said Lou, chuckling.

By 10am, the shop was bustling and busy.

It was starting to warm up outside. You could hear a dull humming from the air conditioner already hard at work. There were three people in the front offices in addition to Jack. Unfortunately, only the offices were air conditioned. Most of the guys in the shop had a big fan at their work station, but it didn't do much. At least one of the bay doors was always open, so you just couldn't cool the shop very well. The shop guys were used to it. No complaints.

Dawn was a large-boned woman with very long very straight brown hair. She sat behind an organized desk located close to the front door. She wore thick glasses, and wasn't what most people would consider pretty. Big woman. Not overweight, just big. She easily stood six feet tall. She complained a lot. Too much sometimes. More than once Jack considered firing her. The main reason he hadn't fired her yet was that he knew she cared about him and his family. Really cared. That, and she had been there a long time and knew how to do everything, and was familiar with all Strong Metal Works clientele. Down the hall, as you walked towards the shop to the right, behind Dawn's reception area and across the hall from Jack's office, there were two men that shared an office. Each had his desk pushed against the wall on opposite sides of the office.

Bill, the sales manager, sat with the phone to his ear. Mid-fifties. Bald on top. Hair around the sides. Looked a little like Friar Tuck, with a medium build. He leaned back in his chair and let out a big laugh. The kind of laugh you charitably give to your brother-in-law when he tells a bad joke. Bill was a little needy, and a certifiable "yes" man, but he could sell. Their sales had gone up every quarter since Jack hired him. Sometimes Jack wondered if he was paying him too much, but so far it'd been worth the gamble. The man sitting on the other side of the room was about half-way through a crossword puzzle. Dick Martin. His feet were propped up on his desk. Jet black hair. Most would consider him ruggedly handsome. Mid thirties. He had a copy of *Seven Habits Of Highly Successful People* on his desk. Pages were dogeared. His origins were humble, but wasn't shy about letting others know he was trying to improve his station. Dick was the shop manager.

"How's your mom, Jack? I mean since her doctor's visit?" asked Dawn from her office.

"Fine. Clean bill." Jack answered from behind his desk.

"You know she still doesn't like it that I took this shop over."

"She likes it. She just feels guilty about it," Dawn responded insightfully.

"She brought it up again this morning. She's still talking about me going to school," Jack said.

"School? What would you go to school for?" Bill asked from his office, having hung up his phone call a moment before.

"He's going to go to school to become a gynecologist. Your wife says she wants to be his first customer," chimed in Dick, still working on his crossword puzzle with his feet on the desk.

This caused Dawn to belt out a loud belly laugh.

"Piss off Dick," quipped Bill.

Dick could hear the sound of Jack's footsteps coming down the hallway towards his office. He quickly took his feet off the desk and put the crossword puzzle he was working on in his drawer.

Jack stopped in the door frame and looked at Dick. "Dick, tell Curtis I want to talk to him please." said Jack, with an eagerness about him.

Dick got up from his chair and started making his way towards the shop, following Jack back down the hall.

"Did I tell you that Curtis and Vin almost got in a fight yesterday out there?" Dick asked Jack before entering the shop.

"No, what happened?" Jack asked as he made his way back into his office, and took a seat behind his desk.

"Vin uses the compressor to clean his station at the end of the day. Blows his dirt and frag onto Curtis's station. Pissed Curtis off. They had words."

"Vin have a suicide wish?" Jack asked. "Curtis has to outweigh Vin by 70 pounds."

"Vin's a pistol. You know that." Dick answered. "Anyway, I talked to them about it."

A few minutes later, Curtis walked into Jack's office. Curtis had red hair. Pale skin with freckles. A bit doughy. Stood around six feet tall. Wore a shirt that said *Strong Metal Works*. Even though most of the men that worked for Jack were older, all gave him respect. Not respect because he was the boss. Respect because he knew most of their jobs better than them, and he was willing to get his hands dirty when the need arose.

"Morning Mr. Strong," Curtis said. "Dick said you wanted to see me."

"I heard you got one of those letters from the government that wanted you to give blood? That right?" Jack asked.

Even though Jack had decided he wasn't going to participate in the Watson Act, he was very curious about it. In fact, he had an insatiable appetite for any information he could get his hands on regarding the government intrusion in people's lives. At least, that is how he perceived it.

"Yes, sir," said Curtis, holding his hat in his hands.

"What happened when you went? What was it like?" Jack asked, studying Curtis' face.

"Wasn't much to it, really. Kinda like going to the doctor. You give them your name. Go in a room. Nurse and a doctor come in and take some blood. Except they don't use a needle. They use this gun looking thing," Curtis explained.

"Gun?"

"Yeah, it just takes a little tiny bit of your blood. Then a little green light came on the end of the gun. Then she said I could go."

"That was it, huh?"

"Yeah, pretty much. Only weird thing was there was this guard stationed there. Toting a gun and stuff. That was kinda weird."

"Why was it weird?" asked Jack, eagerly awaiting Curtis' response.

"Well, other than the fact there was an armed guard at a doctor's office, he had kind of droned out look on his face. Plus, he wasn't toting a pistol. He was carrying an AR 15."

"Droned out huh?" said Jack, taking in what Curtis had just told him. The image of the man at the 7-Eleven this morning jumped into his mind. He had a droned out look.

"And, they just told you that you could leave? Just like that?"

"Yes, sir."

"Did they ever mention why they were taking your blood?" Jack asked.

"No, but I didn't ask neither," Curtis said with a Texas twang.

"All right, buddy. Thanks. Get back to work," Jack said.

He heard Curis walk down the hall. Shortly afterward the door to the shop opened and closed.

Dawn piped up from her office loud enough for Jack to hear. Clearly she had been listening to the conversation between Curtis and Jack. "You didn't tell me you got another letter. Is that what that was about?"

"Yeah. Came yesterday."

"What's it going to take for you to just go up there and get it over with?"

"Doesn't it strike you as crazy wrong that the government asks people to do that?"

"You're going to get in trouble if you don't. Just do it, and get it over with."

Dick chimed in from the room down the hall. "My cousin knows a guy in Austin that refused to go in for that shot. He said eventually two thugs and a nurse lady showed up at this guys house, held him down, and took his blood. After they took his blood, they gun butted him in the head. He's still not right from it. Tell me that's not screwed up?"

"Good lord!" Donna exclaimed.

A few seconds later, Curtis poked his head back in the office and said "tamale truck is here."

For the last four years, at least once a month the tamale lady pulled her truck up to the shop. It had almost become a tradition, and Jack allowed and even participated in the monthly trip out to the tamale truck. After all, the lady's tamales were legendary. And, he thought it created a positive camaraderie for the shop and the office to commingle a little bit. A couple minutes later, most of the shop had been served and were enjoying their tamale's.

Jack stepped up to the truck. The tiny spanish lady looked at Jack and said, "Uno que no se puede romper! El Protector!"

"Wait, what did she call you?" Dawn asked, loud enough so the whole group could hear.

Jack looked a little sheepish. Curtis spoke up. "Last year Jack let this lady read his palm. Ever since then she's been calling him that. Art, ask her why she calls him that."

Arturo Moyeda had been working for Strong Metal Works for seven years. He threw his tamale wrapper in the trash and stepped up to the woman and spoke to her in spanish. She answered him

16

while making a hand gesture towards Jack, and then she did the sign of the cross.

Art said, "She says you are the one that can't be broken. The great protector. A person that will save others and protect the world. She says Jack's hand shows it."

Jack looked down at his hand, and let out a little chuckle. As if anyone could discern such a thing from someone's hand. He really regretted the open airing of the tamale ladies hand reading to almost the entirety of the shop, and the front office staff. He imagined the "El Protector" label will be the source of much ribbing from Dick and Bill especially.

"Okay, everybody. ...El Protector says back to work," Jack said with a smile.

Chapter 4

Jack was sitting on a stool bellied up to the counter overlooking the kitchen in Dottie's Diner. He had been there for about twenty minutes. He was still working on a half-eaten plate of chicken and mashed potatoes. Dotties Diner was smallish. L shaped. Jack always sat at the front bar, because most of the time he ate alone, and it just seemed like the right place to eat, as opposed to one of the red cushioned booths that ran the entire length of the diner. Most important to Jack was that it was around the corner from his shop. Easy. Quick. Most of the lunch crowd had cleared out by now. Jack usually ate late lunches. He ate when he got hungry. Never on a regular schedule.

Melba, a short and overweight waitress, stood in front and just to the side of Jack behind the counter. She had her back to Jack, leaning up against the counter with her arms folded over her massive breasts. Both of them were watching a smallish color television sitting next to a pot of coffee on the counter under the service window to the kitchen. Jack could see the President of the United States speaking to a group behind a podium. The volume was turned down. Jack didn't care. He didn't really like the president. Didn't vote for him. Thought the country was going to shit.

"You know what's weird about him?" said Melba to Jack without turning around to address Jack directly.

"Hmm?" grunted Jack, while chewing his chicken.

"You remember when he was first elected he smiled a lot? Now he has this droned out look on his face all the time. He never smiles anymore."

Now that Jack thought about it, she was right. He hadn't seen the President smile in quite some time. Seemed like at least a couple of years. Jack surmised that he didn't notice this because he flat out didn't like the guy, and tuned out whenever he saw his face on a television. However, now that he looked at him he had the same glassy eyed blank stare that the guy at 7-eleven had this morning. Again, Jack had the same feeling wash over him that there was more to all of this than meets the eye.

"You think it's finally getting to him?" Jack asked just to be conversational. He felt he owed that to Melba. After all, he had been coming to this diner for years, and he couldn't remember a time that Melba wasn't working there. Even though they weren't close friends, there was friendship equity there that Jack respected.

"I just think it's weird. Somethings not right about it. Everything's going to shit," said Melba as she spit a little bit of tobacco juice into a plastic water bottle she kept under the counter. A sight which would turn the stomach of the average patron at any diner, but Jack was used to Melba dipping, and she kept it on the down low for the most part, only dipping in front of seasoned customers like Jack.

"Whaddya gonna do?" Jack asked without looking up. Moments later, Jack finally looked up because of the silence and lack of acknowledgement from Melba. He could see her eyes were fixed on two patrons in the back of the restaurant.

"You see that guy?" Melba whispered to Jack. Jack noticed a thirty-something guy eating with a woman, who looked roughly the same age. He didn't recognize them. They looked like a couple. A married couple, Jack figured due to the fact that they were largely ignoring each other.

"Both of them, the man and the woman have that same weird vacant stare the president had," Melba said.

It's true. The man was facing his wife, but wasn't looking at her. He looked to be fixed on a spot on the wall behind her. Unblinking.

19

He stared, and stared, and kept staring. The woman also was staring, but she appeared to be staring at Jack and Melba. To Jack, this was more than just a coincidence. This morning with the 7-eleven guy, and the president, and now these people. Same vacant stare. What did it mean?

"Tell me that's not creepy as hell!" Melba whispered out of the side of her mouth.

"I'll have to agree with you on that one," said Jack, looking back at the woman staring at him. Jack had the sense that something was really wrong with her.

At this moment, Jack noticed a black Monte Carlo parked along the street adjacent to the diner. The windows were heavily tinted. Couldn't really tell if someone was in the car or not. He only noticed it this time because he had seen the same car parked down the block from his shop earlier this morning, and down the road from his house yesterday. La Marque wasn't a big town, Jack knew most of the everyday cars of people because most people kept to similar schedules, so you would see them and their vehicles at the same time of day. Jack's dad had many "sayings" he would like to use, and Jack was fond of one of them in particular, because there was a lot of truth to it. One time is an occurrence. Twice is a coincidence. Three times you got a problem. This black Monte Carlo just triggered the "you got a problem" stage.

Suddenly Jack felt a tap on his shoulder. He turned to see Karen Faulkner smiling big behind him. He got up so fast his belt clipped the end of the fork he had set on the edge of his plate, and it fell with a clang to the ground. A giant smile broke out on his face to match the one on Karen's face.

"Hey Karen!" said Jack, as he gave her a big hug. After a moment, Karen was ready to break the hug off, but Jack kept going with it, so she did too. She didn't seem to mind. Hugging Jack was always such a comfort to her. It was obvious to anyone that saw them that she had strong feelings for Jack.

Karen was tall for a woman. About 5'9". Long silky blond straight hair. Her skin glowed. She was a beautiful woman. Infectious smile. She wore a University of Missouri Tennis Team shirt, and white shorts.

"Sit down," Jack said, as he motioned to the seat next to him.

Melba the waitress made her way off to check on the other customers in the diner. She figured Jack was done talking to her now that Karen showed up. Jack stole a quick look and noticed the woman in the back was still staring in his direction. He decided not to mention it to Karen. It was just weird, and Jack didn't want to ruin this moment with Karen. But, honestly he couldn't really get it out of his mind.

"It's good to see you!" said Karen.

"It's good to see you! A sight for sore eyes," Jack said emphatically.

Jack yelled across the deli to Melba. "Melba, iced tea for Karen please." Melba looked up and nodded her head without saying anything.

"You look great! How are you? How was school?" said Jack, talking fast.

"I'm exhausted, and ready for this semester to be over," said Karen, letting out a big exhale with her tongue out.

"I haven't heard much from you lately. You must have been busy. How have things been going?" asked Jack, with the slightest bit of nervous anticipation.

Karen smiled. "Well let's see. Yes, I'm actually engaged to a medical student."

"Engaged?" said Jack, trying to mask his shock and disappointment.

"Yes, he's from Europe. He was a male model for a few years, and then he decided to go to medical school. He's going to be a heart surgeon."

Jack paused for a moment, trying to detect if Karen was joking.

"You are such a big fat liar!" said Jack with a relieved smile.

Karen reached over and punched Jack in the arm.

"You're still my guy, dope!. Know this, Jack I go to school with a bunch of boys. You, you are a man," said Karen, as she placed her hand on Jack's arm.

"So, why did you come home early?" asked Jack, with a bit of a hopeful tone.

"As my grandma is fond of saying, I had a 'hankering' to come home and see my family, and see you Jack. I missed you."

"I missed you too," said Jack, looking into Karen's eyes.

"How did you know I was at the diner?" said Jack, smiling.

"Dawn told me. I went by the office."

"You went to the office just to see me?" asked Jack, as he pressed his palm to his chest.

"Yes I did," said Karen grinning. "Your mom told my mom that you were about to get thrown in jail because you haven't gone by to give blood yet. So, my mom told me to go to your office and make you go to the place so you can give blood. Plus it was a good excuse to see you."

Melba sat a glass of tea in front of Karen, and then returned to her position, her back to Jack and Karen, watching television.

"My mom called your mom huh? Well, I guess I have no choice now. I gotta go."

"Once I'm on the job, you know stuff gets done," said Karen, as she reached over and patted Jack on the leg.

"Let's go tomorrow, though. I have to get a job finished and shipped out to Lyondell today. How about tomorrow morning?"

"Let's do it! Now that we have that settled, there's something else I want to talk to you about..."

Chapter 5

Jack got home from the shop at 5:41pm. His mom was just putting the finishing touches on dinner. Pork chops, corn, and mashed potatoes. Jack loved the smell of pork chops, especially his mom's. When Jack entered the kitchen, June was standing over the oven. His little brother Jimmy was standing by the back door looking out the window. He had a Superman action figure in his hand, but he was fixed on something outside. Jimmy gave Jack a quick glance and motioned for him to come over and look out the back window. Jack lifted the blinds and peaked out.

"Look! It's the coyote I was telling you about!" said Jimmy excitedly.

Jack could see their giant bull Blue looking down at a coyote. The coyote was standing inside Blue's pen, about six feet away from him. The coyote glanced up at Blue. The giant bull gave a fleeting glance at the coyote, and then turned it's head and continued munching on it's hay.

"That coyote is crazy," said Jack, with a bit of a chuckle. "That's what I was telling you Jimmy. Blue knows that coyote can't hurt him. He's not worried about him. He might as well be a rock."

"Go wash up, Jimmy. We are about to eat," said June, putting her dish towel down, and wiping her forehead with the back of her left hand.

Looking at his mom, Jack walked over to the kitchen sink and began washing his hands. Jimmy ran down the hall into the bathroom. Jack looked over his shoulder to make sure Jimmy had left the room before he started talking.

"Hey Mom, I saw Karen today."

"Oh really! I talked to her mom earlier."

"Yeah, I know she told me you did. We're gonna go to do the blood thing at the government office tomorrow. So, you win I guess."

"Oh good! I know you didn't want to, but I was just scared for you."

Jack turned and faced his mom as he dried his hands with a dish towel.

"Mom, she mentioned something else to me I wanted to ask you about..."

"Yes?"

"She had a genealogy project she's been working on this semester at school. She picked our family for the project. It's where you go back and map several generations of a family on a flow chart. As far back as you can go..."

"She did?" Jack saw a fleeting panic race across his mom's face before she quickly regained her composure. She laid the paring knife she had been using to cut a bell pepper down on the island. Her hand trembled. She seemed suddenly addled.

"Yeah. She said she was actually able to go back several generations. Seven generations on dad's side, before things started to dry up."

"Jimmy, hurry up now," June called, almost trying not to hear what Jack was saying about genealogy.

"She said she only had one problem. She couldn't find any records for me. No birth records. No adoption records. It's like one day I just appeared on the scene. ...Mom, is there anything you need to tell me about all this?" asked Jack, with a note of anger in his voice.

"What?" asked June in a worried defeated manner. "I don't know what she's talking about."

"Mom!"

"We..."

"Mom, tell me!" said Jack, raising his voice.

"We weren't supposed to say anything. They said they would take care of everything." June sat down at the table and started to cry.

"Mom, I'm not mad at you. I just need to know what's going on. What do you mean? If I'm not your son, who's son am I? How did you get me?" Jack's questions raced out of his mouth.

"I told your dad before he died we should tell you, but he didn't want to. He said it was too dangerous."

"Dangerous? What? What do you mean? Why would it be dangerous?" Jack demanded.

"Someone from your dad's past reached out to him. I don't even know who it was. It was someone from before I knew your dad. He went out of town for two days. When he came back he had you with him." June said as she reached for a napkin to wipe her eyes.

"He told me that we were going to raise you as our son, and for me never to mention any of it to anyone. He said if anyone ever asked, we would just tell them we adopted you. You were only a couple of months old. A sweet little baby boy..."

Just then, Jimmy walked back into the kitchen.

"I was washing my hands, and then I took the quickest poop of my life..." He saw his mom sitting at the kitchen table crying, and his brother in an obviously stressed state.

"Whaaaat did I miss?" Jimmy hesitantly inquired.

Chapter 6

Jack couldn't sleep that night. The idea that his whole self-image of who he was, and where he was from was not accurate just stopped him down. Who were his real mom and dad? Where are they? Why did they give him up? Why was it in such a hurry, and such a big secret? The entire foundation his life was built on became unhinged. It was just an endless loop that played in Jack's mind. The more he thought about it the angrier he got. Mainly angry at his mother and father for keeping such a gigantic secret from him. This news was a toxic punch of stress for Jack's mind and body. He felt hot, and couldn't stop sweating. Finally, after hours laying in bed thinking about it, Jack decided upon a course of action. One that hopefully would keep him more even keeled, and in control of things. Jack's dad always used to tell him that stress was born from feeling that you didn't have control over something. So, he decided to just focus on what he had control over, and try not to worry about things he didn't have control over. Before Jack realized it, his alarm was going off. He didn't sleep a wink.

"I just can't believe it," said Karen, after hoping in Jack's truck a moment earlier. Jack had just quickly summarized the conversation with his mother. "I hope I didn't... I mean I didn't want to start a family thing. I just wanted you to know what I found. I guess I should have thought more before I dropped that bomb on you."

"I don't know if it's a 'family thing,' but it's definitely something ...it's definitely a thing. It's a pretty big enchilada," said Jack as he turned the corner onto Main Street.

"Anyway, she's still mom to me. Secrets or no secrets."

Jack pulled up in front of the government blood center. It was about halfway down Main Street. Karen sat next to him. It was ten minutes to ten in the morning. There was a stenciled name on the exterior of the building, *National Compliance Center* in big red letters. The rest of the exterior was white. The Compliance Center was in the middle of six shops on the east side of main street. Each one side to side. Next door was a shoe shop, and on the other side was Rick's Barber Shop. Jack could see Rick through the window cutting a head of hair. He realized he was overdue for a hair cut himself.

Suddenly, down the street Jack saw the same black Monte Carlo he had been seeing for the past couple of days parked in front of a Church's Fried Chicken. He thought to himself, *could I just be imagining how weird this is?* He wished he hadn't seen it. He was already a little uneasy about going into this center in the first place.

"Well, you ready?" Karen asked, smiling.

Jack looked at her and gave a little failed smile. He then exhaled like he was resigned to it. "Yeah, let's do it."

Inside the building it was similar to any doctor's office you might visit. Reception area. Ten chairs staged in an efficient manner throughout the room. Few tables with magazines on them. Little glass sliding window at the end of the room, with a door next to it. The door presumably led to medical rooms. There were two young men already sitting in two of the chairs.

Jack immediately realized that there was one notable exception to a normal doctor's waiting room. There was a man in an all black military tactical gear standing next to the glass windows. He stood looking straight ahead with a blank glassy eyed stare on his face. An AR-15 in his arms. The two young men sitting in the waiting room were checking Karen out until they saw Jack looking at them, then they quickly averted their stares. Karen sat down in the chair closest to the windows. Jack had his eyes fixed on the military man as he walked up to the window and tapped on it. A few seconds later, a forty-something woman in a nurses outfit slid the small glass door open. Her face was pockmarked, and the outfit she was wearing was at least a size too small for her. *Fake blond hair, and way too much makeup,* Jack thought.

"Do you have your letter?" the woman asked in a husky perturbed voice.

"Yes, ma'am. I have it somewhere here." Jack started to rifle through his pockets.

He heard Karen give a small whistle, and looking back at her, he saw she had his letter. *Karen was always so prepared*, Jack thought. Jack took the letter from Karen and handed it to the woman behind the counter. Without a peep, the woman took the letter and shut the glass door with a thud.

Walking back to his chair, he could hear the large woman talking to someone behind the glass. "I've got you beat so far today, Ginny. This one is on his fifth notice."

Jack sat down next to Karen. Leaning over, he whispered into her ear. "Did you hear that?"

"Yes," said Karen, fighting back a laugh. "You're in big trouble mister."

"I'm telling you, I have a bad feeling about this place." Jack continued to study the soldier in the corner. *Why doesn't he blink? How can he stand in that position for so long without moving?* Jack motioned towards the soldier with his head while looking at Karen.

"Tell me that's not weird."

"Relax! It will all be over soon," said Karen, squeezing Jack's arm. "It's no big deal."

Thirty minutes later, Jack found himself sitting at the end of the examination table. His legs dangled over the edge. Despite their best efforts the nurse wouldn't allow Karen to come into the room with Jack. So, there he sat. Alone. Wondering why he was having to sit on this table and give some of his blood to the government. *What did they want with it? Why were they making young men all over the country come into offices just like this one and give their blood? Why not women? Just men. Why?* It didn't make any sense!

After another ten minutes, a man and a woman entered the room. The man was about five feet eight inches tall. Dark hair. Looked to be in his mid-thirties. He wore a long white coat over his white shirt and wrinkled tan pants. The woman was young. Dressed in a nurses outfit. Dark hair pinned up into a bun behind her head. She moved in a jerky, nervous fashion. Smallish. Pale skin. Couldn't have been more than five two.

"Hello," Jack said.

"Good morning Mr. Strong. I'm Doctor Roberts," said the Doctor as he was looking down at Jack's file. "Why did you wait until letter number five to come in?"

"Honestly, I just didn't like the whole idea of the test. Still don't."

"What made you finally come in?"

"My mom was worried I would get into trouble with the government."

"Your mom is smart ...just looking out for you. Don't all mom's do that?" said the doctor as he gave Jack a quick small smile. "Judy, can you get the gun for me?"

The young nurse nervously whipped around and pulled open a drawer in one of the cabinets against the wall and removed what looked like an oversized dart gun. It had two LED bulbs on the side. One red, and one green. She handed it to the doctor.

"Would you mind telling me why they want to test my blood?" asked Jack.

"We aren't allowed to discuss that. I'm sorry. In truth I don't even know. ...I just do what they tell me," answered the doctor matter-of-factly.

The doctor held the gun up in front of Jack. "This is what we use to take a blood sample from you. The test mechanism is inside the gun. So, it will check your blood. This little light will turn green, and then we'll be done."

"Soooo, that's it huh?" Jack inquired.

"Yep, takes about twenty seconds."

"Please hold out your arm," said the nurse in a mousey high-pitched voice. Jack held his arm out. The nurse took a small alcohol swab and rubbed a space on his forearm halfway between his hand and elbow. The doctor then placed the tip of the gun firmly on the spot the nurse had just rubbed with alcohol. He saw the doctor pull the trigger, and felt a small prick on his arm.

A brief moment later the red light flashed brightly on the side of the gun.

"I thought you said it was going to be green?" asked Jack in a concerned tone.

The doctor stared at the red flashing light on the side of the gun, his mouth open slightly. Not believing what he was seeing. He looked towards the nurse.

"Have you ever seen red before?" the nurse Judy asked the doctor in a panicky fast-paced voice.

"No. ...No I haven't. Never heard of one either. It's got to be a mistake." The doctor went over to the cabinets against the far wall of the room, opened a drawer, and removed another gun. He grabbed Jack's arm, put the new gun against his arm and again pulled the trigger.

Jack felt the same prick to his skin. A moment later. ...A red flashing light.

The doctor laid the gun down on the table next to Jack. He took a step back and looked at Jack, but almost like he was looking through Jack. Processing his thoughts. Thinking about what he was supposed to do now. Going through procedures and protocol in his mind.

He looked over at the nurse. "You can go now, Judy."

Judy gave a concerned look to Jack, and then reverted her gaze back to the doctor. She gripped her clipboard tightly against her chest, turned on her heel, and walked out the door, shutting it behind her.

Brett Sampson

"What happens now?" asked Jack, exasperated and concerned.

The doctor calmly walked over next to the door. He pushed a button on the intercom next to the wall and spoke. "Initiate protocol one."

This wasn't just a message to the nurse at the desk. His voice went out over speakers all over the office. Jack could hear his voice reverberating down the hall.

The doctor then held out his hand. "Give me your cell phone Mr. Strong."

"Piss off. You can't have my cell phone! Can someone please tell me what the hell is going on?" Jack stood up and faced the doctor, standing at least a head taller than him.

"I'm serious! You guys are pissing me off. What is going on?!" Jack's voice was rising, angry.

The doctor swiftly turned and exited the office. Jack could hear a deadbolt lock turn on the door to the office.

"What the hell is going on?" Jack asked himself as he tried to open the door he knew would be locked.

Jack heard a lot of shuffling and knocking sounds down the hall outside the door. Then he could hear Karen's voice.

"I'm going back there. Get out of my way," she said, her voice panicky. Loud. Then he heard a slap, and Karen screaming.

"Karen! You bastards!" Jack reared back and tried to kick the door to the examination room down. A few seconds later, the door opened and the soldier from the waiting room entered the room, his assault rifle pointed at Jack's head.

"Are you the one that hit her!" Jack screamed as he approached the soldier.

The soldier took the butt of his gun, and slammed it into the side of Jack's head. Jack went down hard. Dazed and woozy on all fours next to the examination table Jack placed one hand on the edge of the table he was just sitting on. He heard a click, followed closely by another click. Looking up, he could see the soldier had handcuffed him to a metal flange on the edge of the table. Jack pulled his arm away and tried to break the flange. It was no use. He was stuck there. His mind slowly began to clear. Jack sat on the floor next to the table with his right arm resting in the air, being held aloft by the handcuffs. He looked up at the soldier, who was standing a few feet away with his gun leveled at Jack's head.

"You got me okay! You can put the gun down now. I'm handcuffed to the fucking table!"

The soldier didn't respond. He just stood still, staring down the barrel of his rifle with a glassy-eyed determined gaze. Down the hall, Jack could hear more commotion. A man's voice - sounded like the doctor's said, "You can't come in here!" Then a smack and a loud thud.

A few seconds later, the door opened. A man in a tan jacket and military colored green pants entered. He had short dark hair, and was carrying a semi-automatic pistol. Both hands on it, in a shooting ready position. He quickly scanned the room. The soldier holding the assault rifle quickly turned the rifle towards the man, but it was too late. The man in the tan jacket fired two quick shots into the soldier's head. So loud, Jack was in shock. His ears were ringing. The soldier fell to the floor like a sack of potatoes. The far wall opposite where the soldier was standing was painted in blood and brains.

Jack made the assumption the man was here for him since he killed the soldier and not him. The tan jacketed man immediately began rifling through the soldier's clothes. Jack presumed he was looking for the key to the handcuffs. Breathing heavy and fast, Jack was in shock. His head was still throbbing from being struck by the soldier a moment earlier.

"Who are you? Why did you kill him? And, why was he pointing his gun at me?" said Jack, exasperated and terrified.

The man took a brief glance at Jack's face before he found the keys to the handcuffs in the soldiers shooting vest.

"I can't believe I found you ...we have to hurry. They will be here inside of ten minutes."

The man unlocked Jack from the handcuffs, leaving the other end of the cuffs dangling from the table. He helped Jack to his feet.

"Wait. What? Who will be here? Who are you?"

"No time. Talk later. Can you walk?" the tan man asked Jack as he put a hand on each of Jack's shoulders and looked him in the eye.

"Yeah. Let's go."

They moved into the hall. It was chaos. There was a red light flashing on and off just outside the examination room Jack had just come from. Papers were strewn all over the floor. The doctor that had just given Jack the blood test was sprawled on the floor unconscious just outside the door to the examination room. Karen was sitting down on the floor of the hallway with her back against the wall just in front of the door that leads to the waiting room. Her hands were on her head. Clearly, she had been struck woozy and was just now regaining her senses. Jack was on her in an instant, helping her to her feet.

"Karen? Karen are you ok? We need to go now." Jack put her arm around his neck and his arm around her waist to help her walk. They quickly made their way through the waiting room, which was now empty. A red flashing light bathed the room in a surreal red glow. On, off, on, off. The man in the tan jacket moved quickly behind Jack and Karen. His hand pressing against Jack's back to hurry him up.

When they breached the front door Jack could see the black Monte Carlo parked right out front. He immediately realized the man in the tan jacket had been watching him for a while now.

"Get in," said the man in the tan jacket. Pointing to his black car.

Jack turned around with Karen still clinging to him.

"Listen buddy, I appreciate what you did for me in there, but I'm leaving in my truck not your car. I don't know who you are. This whole thing is fucking insane!"

"No! Listen, you have no idea how important you are. You are in danger. I need to tell you things..."

Just then there was a loud gunshot. The man in the tan jacket winced in pain. Looking back at the door to the clinic Jack could see the big rude nurse that had been behind the glass standing in the doorway with the soldier's assault rifle. The man in the tan jacket had just been shot in the back by the nurse. He immediately wheeled around and discharged one round of his pistol hitting the nurse in the forehead. She dropped to the ground instantly, dead. He then dropped to one knee. Looking at Jack with a scared desperate look on his face, the tan jacketed man was hopelessly trying to reach around to the spot he was shot with his non-pistoled hand.

Jack spun around and quickly helped Karen into the front passenger seat of his truck. He then ran back and slung the man's arm around his neck and helped him into the back seat of the truck. Jack pushed the wounded man's feet into the cab and shut the door. Looking down at this blood covered hands, Jack couldn't comprehend what had transpired in the last two minutes. It just didn't make any sense. Back in the cab, Jack hit the gas and his Ford truck responded with screeching tires and smoke. He was gone. Jack looked around at the man in the tan jacket. He was laying down on the back seat. Blood everywhere.

"You all right back there? We need to get you to a hospital." Jack said, in a panicked tone.

"No! Just pull over somewhere safe. Somewhere quiet. Somewhere you wouldn't normally go. I, I need to talk to you," said the man in the tan jacket. He was in obvious pain, and trying to stay conscious.

"You all right?" Jack asked Karen.

"Yes, I think so. That soldier hit me," said Karen, as her hands trembled.

"Well, he got his. He won't be hitting anyone anymore."

Jack wondered for a moment where he could take the man in his back seat. Somewhere quiet the man said. Then Jack remembered his best friend from high school, Teddy. Teddy's dad had a small auto repair shop just east of downtown, no more than a few minutes from where they were now. He remembered Teddy telling him his dad had to leave town a few days ago because his sister had died, and his dad had to make arrangements for her. She lived in Port Arthur, Texas. Jack knew the funeral was set for today, so the shop should be empty.

Having been to the shop on numerous occasions Jack knew where they kept a spare key. Jack drove around to the back of the shop so his truck couldn't be seen from the street. Once inside, he opened one of the big bay doors where his truck was parked, and then pulled his truck into the shop. Closing the big door to the shop behind him, Jack opened the door to the rear cab and the man looked unconscious.

"This is crazy. I've got to get this guy to a hospital," said Jack.

"No!" said the man in the tan jacket lying completely prone in the back seat without opening his eyes. "No hospitals. Get…, get me out of here."

Jack helped the man from the truck into a chair that Teddy's dad kept tucked into a desk against the far wall of the shop. The man took a firm grip of the side of the desk with his right hand, and his left clutched the cracked cushion of the chair he was sitting in. He winced in pain.

"Where are we?" The tan jacketed man asked.

"It's safe. No one's going to come here," said Jack. "Can you please explain why this is happening to me?"

The tan jacketed man took several short breaths, before he attempted to speak. "You aren't who you think you are. You were genetically modified before you were born as part of a military experiment to create a weapon that can't be defeated. It was called Project Density."

Jack looked at Karen in disbelief. Karen attempted to hand the man a small cup of water. He waved her off.

"Wait, what?" Jack asked, confused and frustrated.

"This whole giving blood thing for men when they reach the age of twenty one was all designed to find you. Shortly after you were born, you were taken from those that held you, and placed with the family you grew up with."

"No way! This is crazy. Besides, I'm not a weapon. I'm just a guy. I'm no different than any other guy. No stronger or faster. I bleed just like any other guy," said an exasperated Jack.

The tan jacketed man reached into his jacket pocket and pulled out a black case. It looked similar to a case you would keep your glasses in. He handed it to Jack as he turned his head to the ground and coughed. Blood spattered on the ground.

Wiping the blood from around his mouth with the sleeve of his tan jacket the man again began to speak. "You are the same as any other guy because your DNA requires a catalyst to affect your change in density."

"What do you mean change in density?"

"That was the goal of the experiment. To increase the density of the subject. In that case is a syringe. If you inject it you will change. Your cells will begin to multiply, but maintain the same space they are in now. You will become more dense. On a scale of 10,000 to 1. Not only that, the hardness of your cells will change too. Similar to a diamond in hardness."

Jack opened the case and saw a syringe with a bluish liquid inside. "What are you saying? That I would turn into the Hulk?"

"No, you will appear like the man you are now. ...but, you will be different. Dense. Heavy, probably weigh thousands of pounds. No weapon will be able to hurt you. Nothing will be able to penetrate your skin."

"You've got to be kidding me." Jack got up and began pacing the floor. "What do you mean, 'probably'?"

"No one really knows what will happen when you inject that syringe, because you are the only one that survived before the program was shut down."

"That's not all," the tan jacketed man said. "It is also believed that your strength will increase as a result of the increase in density. It's hard to say by how much, though. You should be incredibly strong."

Jack looked at Karen. "Do you believe any of this? Do you think it's for real?"

"After the last fifteen minutes, I think I do," said Karen as she took the syringe case from Jack to have a look for herself.

The man in the tan jacket bent over to cough again; again blood. This time he fell out of the chair and sprawled on the floor, his face wrinkled in agony.

"Come on, Karen, help me get him into the truck. We need to take him to see a doctor."

"Listen!" The man grabbed Jack by the arm.

"My assignment was to find you and bring you to my commanding officer. I can't do that now, so you will have to find him yourself."

The tan jacketed man reached inside his jacket and pulled out a white card. "This card has an address on it. Go there. There is a payphone on the corner of this building. Dial four sevens, and await further instruction." The man began to cough again. Again in agony; spitting up blood.

"Lose the girl. You can't go anywhere. They will kill anyone and everyone you know to get to you. They know who you are now and where you live."

"What do you mean they will kill who I know?"

The eyes of the man in the tan jacket closed. His body went completely limp. Jack bent down and started shaking his shoulders. Slapped his face.

"What do you mean they will kill who I know?!"

"Is he breathing?" asked Karen.

"Not sure. I can't feel a pulse." Jack answered.

Jack looked up at Karen, who was still holding the cup of water she had attempted to give the dying man. "I've got to go home to check on mom and Jimmy. If they're all right, they could be in danger."

"I'm scared, Jack," said Karen, as she put her hand on Jack's arm.

Jack took the water from Karen's hand and set it on the table, and then gave her a big protective embrace.

"Don't worry. I'm not sure what's happening, but I won't let anything happen to you."

"Are you going to inject that syringe?" Karen asked.

"Hell no! Besides, you heard him say that they really aren't sure how it would affect me anyway. Might just kill me. I do have to check on Mom and Jimmy though."

Jack started to walk towards the driver's side of the truck.

"Are we just going to leave this dead man in Teddy's dad's shop?" Karen asked, looking down at the bloody corpse of the man in the tan jacket.

"I would call the sheriff's office and let them know he was here, but I'm not sure who I can trust at the moment, so I think we should just leave him here for now," said Jack, as he slipped the black case containing the syringe into his back pocket and got into the truck. Karen jumped in beside him. They were off.

Chapter 7

Fourteen minutes later Jack and Karen arrived at Jack's home. Slowing on his approach to the turn off for their driveway, Jack pulled his truck off the road next to a long row of big bushy cedar trees. His dad had planted the row of trees over fifteen years ago to give them some privacy. If there was someone at his home, Jack didn't want them to know that he had just arrived.

"You stay in the truck until I come and get you. If there is someone at the house, I don't want you to get hurt."

"No, Jack, I want to come with you," Karen said, half scared and half mad that he wouldn't allow her to come along.

"Absolutely not! You stay here! You saw at the clinic what these people are capable of." Jack gently closed the door to his truck, and made his way over to a small gap between two of the trees. He slowly peered around a branch, and could see the entire house. Only car he could see was his mom's Honda Civic. No other sign of visitation. No vehicles. Nothing. All was quiet.

Jack sprinted to the front door of his home, which was a ranch-style one story L-shaped house. There was a three-car detached garage to the left side of the home as you looked at the house from the street. Behind the home was a big red barn, the pen they kept the bull Blue in, and behind that about ten acres of fenced area they kept a few cows in. Even though the trip from the road to the house was about one hundred yards, Jack felt like he had covered it in mere seconds. Jack quietly looked through the window next to the front door to see if he could see anyone. Nothing. He slowly opened the front door, which was unlocked. It was always unlocked during the day. The front door opened into the living room. All quiet. No one, no sign of a struggle.

"Mom?" Jack said in a hopeful voice.

Walking through the living room and turning into the kitchen, again, Jack saw nothing. Looked like his mom must have been making something, because there were chopped onions on the cutting board. He walked closer to the island where his mom had been working. Then he saw her...

He could just see her feet on the ground around the corner of the kitchen island. Jack quickly made the two big steps needed to get a full view of where she was. June Strong was laying in a pool of her own blood, face down. She had been shot in the head.

"Noooo!!" Jack's eyes filled with tears. He knelt down in the pool of blood that surrounded his mother's lifeless body and put his hands on her back. "No, no, no, no! Mom, no. No. No!" For a moment he silently wept over his mom's body, eyes tightly shut, his tears streaming down his cheeks and falling onto his mom's back. Then his head shot up.

"Jimmy!" Jack shot up like a lightning bolt, and started looking around the rest of the house calling Jimmy's name. "Jimmy? Jimbo?" He looked through each bedroom at a frantic pace, unaware or uncaring that whoever shot his mother might still be hanging around. Jack walked to the back door and looked out the glass to see what he could see outside. Nothing. He opened the back door and stepped out onto the porch. Looking to his right, he could see his little brother lying on the ground next to the tractor in front of the barn.

"Oh god no!" Jack sprinted to his brother's body. "No, no, no, no, no, no, no! Not Jimmy. Not my little brother. For fucks sake he's just a kid!" Jack knelt and cradled Jimmy's head between his knees. Tears streamed down his cheeks. Jimmy had been shot in the chest and was laying on his back. There was a small Superman action figure a few inches away from his right hand. Jack rocked back and forth.

"Jimmy, Jimmy, Jimmy, no Jimmy, no Jimmy, no, no, no."

At that moment Jack heard the crack of a gunshot. Simultaneously it felt as if someone had hit him with a baseball bat in his right shoulder. The energy from the impact with the bullet caused him to fall over backward. Jack immediately rolled over onto his stomach and pushed himself up with the arm that hadn't been shot. He staggered to his feet.

He could see a single man in a black suit. White shirt. Black tie. The man walked out of the detached garage with a hand gun trained on Jack.

"You killed my family."

"Yes, I did," said the man in the black suit. His eyes didn't have that glassy blank gaze like the soldier in the blood clinic. His eyes were clear. Calm. "It's nothing personal. Just carrying out orders."

"You fucking bastard!" Jack started to slowly stagger backwards, trying to circle around the other side of the tractor to take him out of the direct line of sight of the assassin.

"That first shot was just to see if you had injected the catalyst. Now that I see you haven't, I'm going to kill you," said the man in the suit calmly.

Jack attempted to make a jump around to the other side of the tractor. Another gunshot. This one hit him in the leg. He fell to the ground on the far side of the tractor. The bullet hit Jack in the left thigh. The pain was searing. He tried to gain more ground between him and the assassin by crawling backward using his elbows. He glanced under the back tire of the tractor and saw a tire iron. Jack grabbed the tire iron and was ready to throw it as soon as the assassin cleared his sight line. He was going to have to throw it with his left hand because his right was not working from the gunshot wound. The man in the black suit cleared the edge of the tractor. Jack let the tire iron fly with as much force as he could muster. The tire iron hit the assassin in the throat. Adrenaline is a funny thing, because the force of his throw caused the tire iron to penetrate about half of it's eighteen inch length into and through the man's throat.

With his free hand, the man grabbed the tire iron sticking out of his neck. He didn't try to pull it out, he just held it. His eyes widened. They were in equal parts surprised and in shock. Then he dropped to his knees. He slowly raised his gun and pointed it towards Jack.

There was nothing Jack could do. He couldn't move. He could only hope the guy lost consciousness before he could pull the trigger. The gun exploded with another discharge, striking Jack squarely in the chest.

Karen was on a dead run from the truck the moment she heard the first gunshot. She rounded the side of the house and the aftermath of the carnage was on full display. Little Jimmy lying on one side of the tractor. Jack and the man in the black suit on the other. No one was moving. They all appeared to be dead, or best case, unconscious. Karen was in a state of shock. As she ran towards Jack, she could see little Jimmy in her left peripheral vision, but couldn't bear to steal a close look of his lifeless body. *Who would kill a child?* she thought.

Jack, by all accounts, looked dead. She knelt down beside him. "Jack! Oh, Jack!" She wept uncontrollably as she turned his head towards her. She opened his eyes. Non-responsive. Blood everywhere. Jack was dead. Then she remembered the man in the tan jacket at Teddy's dad's auto shop. She remembered the syringe. *Maybe that was Jack's only hope,* she thought. Where was the syringe? She felt for the case in his front pockets. Nothing. Then she reached around to feel his back pockets. Yes! There it was. Quickly, she pulled the case out, opened it up, and removed the syringe containing the strange blue liquid. Without any further thought, she plunged the needle into his shoulder and pushed the blue liquid into his veins.

She then stood up and took a half-step back. "Come on, Jack. Come on, come on, come on..."

She stood there for at least a minute, and there was nothing. No movement, nothing. Then, she thought she could hear something. A very low frequency sound, like a low low hum that seemed to be coming from Jack's body. A brief second later, Jack's eyes shot open, and he took the biggest breath any man has ever taken. It seemed Jack's body was determined to make this transformation, bullets or no bullets. Jack rolled over onto his stomach and pushed himself up with his fists. His face was still just inches off the ground. He let out a long loud scream, the low frequency humming sound still emanating from his body. Except it was louder now. Jack let out another scream and pounded the ground with his fist.

"Jack, you okay?" Karen asked, concerned.

Jack shot her a look. The whites of his eyes were blood red. Something was really going on inside his body. "Get back," he said in a voice so deep, so guttural, it frightened her.

The low-frequency hum continued to grow louder. Again, Jack pounded the ground with his fists and screamed. Then he brought his arms in close to him, his fists against his chest, hunched over. He continued to scream, and it looked as if he was contracting every muscle in his body simultaneously. Then Karen had the strangest sensation. Even though she was standing five or six feet away from Jack, she felt she was being pulled towards him. She was having to lean back against an invisible force in order to not be pulled towards him, even then she was still inching closer to him. But, it wasn't just her. The dead man lying on the ground about eight feet away from him also started to slide towards Jack as if being pulled by an invisible rope. Even the tractor next to him started to inch towards

Jack. Suddenly, Karen realized that as Jack was contracting all his muscles he was generating his own gravitational field. Tiny rocks from the ground around Jack were flying up and sticking to Jack's body. The humming sound coming from Jack's body continued to grow louder. It almost had a grinding tenor to the sound now, like thousands of rocks rubbing together. Then... silence. The humming sound stopped. The rocks that were stuck to him dropped off. Karen no longer felt the invisible force pulling her towards Jack. He had relaxed his muscles, and remained on his knees, hunched over.

Jack looked up at Karen. His eyes weren't blood red anymore. They were normal. He felt the wound on his shoulder and leg ...they were healed.

"Are you okay, Karen?" Jack asked.

"Yes, I am. What about you?"

"I, I don't know. I think so." Jack looked down at his hand. He opened it wide, made a fist, and then opened it again. "I feel weird. You gave me that shot?"

Karen nodded her head. "I did. You seemed like you were dead. I didn't think I had a choice. I'm sorry Jack. I didn't know what else to do."

"It's okay," said Jack, remembering the pain of the gun shots just moments before.

"What do you feel like? Are you different? Like that guy said you would be?"

"I'm not sure." Jack stood up. He turned around and looked at the dead man with the tire iron sticking out of his neck. "That guy killed my family. He killed mom and little Jimmy." Jack was fighting back tears. "He said he was given orders to kill them."

Jack walked around to the front of the tractor so he could see Jimmy's body on the ground. For a brief moment, he had hoped he had just imagined Jimmy was dead. No, his little brother was still lying there on the ground. Jack placed both hands on the front of the tractor, turned his head and cried into his left biceps. After a moment, Jack stopped crying. His hands still on the tractor, he looked at the ground.

"I'm going to find out who did this, who ordered this, and I'm going to dish out some justice!" Jack said. Then he gazed up from the ground to the tractor. His look was steely determination mixed with anger and agonizing sadness. He gave the tractor a shove.

Karen couldn't believe what she was seeing. The tractor, which must have weighed at least three thousand pounds shot back through the open door to the barn, and then burst through the wall on the far side, ending up in the field just beyond the barn. She looked back at Jack, who was looking down at his hands in disbelief.

"I guess he was right about you getting stronger," Karen said.

Jack looked at Karen. "I don't know what I am right now. I'll figure it out. You need to get out of here, though."

"What? No, I want to be here with you ...to help you." Karen put her hand on Jack's arm.

"My whole family just got killed by these people. Do you think they would hesitate to kill you if they knew we were friends? Hell, they probably already know. You take your mom and dad and go up to your fishing cabin for a while. You can take my truck."

"What are you going to do?" Karen asked.

Jack pulled his phone out of his pocket. "First I'm going to call the Sheriff and get them to help me with mom and Jimmy. Then, I'm gonna find out who ordered my family to be killed, and kill them."

"I thought we couldn't trust the sheriff's department?" Karen asked, remembering what Jack had said in Teddy's dad's garage.

"They've already killed my family. They can't kill them again. I need to get them taken care of, and make sure they have proper arrangements."

"What if they send someone else to try to kill you while you're still here?" Karen asked.

Jack bent down and picked up the gun the dead man was using. He pointed it at the palm of his hand and fired. There was a metallic ricochet sound. Karen jumped. The sound startled her. Jack presented the palm of his hand to Karen. No wound. Not even a mark on his hand.

"They can't hurt me now ...but they can get hurt."

Chapter 8

Over the course of the next three hours, scores of people from the sheriff's department and emergency services scoured over Jack's home. Jack was on the lookout for that glassy-eyed vacuous look he had come to recognize as someone that wasn't in control of what they were doing. Someone governed by someone or something else. Like the guard in the clinic. Luckily, he didn't see anyone with that look.

The deputy grilled him for two hours. About the clinic, about his home. Why was he being targeted for killing? Since there were witnesses and camera footage at the clinic that proved no wrongdoing by Jack, the sheriff had to give Jack a pass. The sheriff didn't like Jack's answer that he didn't know who or what was trying to kill him, but he had no choice. He had to take Jack's word for it. The sheriff also didn't like Jack's refusal to sit down at a table for the questioning, but Jack was trying to hide the fact that he now weighed several thousand pounds. He knew if he sat in a chair, the chair would break. He also refused a medic's attempt to check him out. He didn't want anyone touching him. He didn't want his secret out.

Before Karen left in Jack's truck to get her parents, he gave her a cell phone he had recently purchased for Jimmy. He told her to turn her cell off, and leave that one on. Her parents had a fishing cabin on Lake Eufaula in Oklahoma, about seven hours north of where they were in La Marque, Texas. That's where they were headed. That was the only safe place Jack could think of sending them.

The medics took his mother, little Jimmy, and the killer to the morgue. For the first time Jack was alone. He sat down on the concrete steps of his back porch and took a deep slow breath. *What a day,* Jack thought. In the span of one day, he had found out there were people trying to kill him, that the mom he thought was his mom wasn't, that he was a weapon that was created in a laboratory, and his family was murdered. Wrapping his head around the loss was impossible. It was almost like it happened to someone else's family. Like it wasn't real yet, even though he knew very well they were dead.

As he sat on the step, Jack began to relax and really feel his body. He felt his right forearm with his left hand. The skin felt the same to him, but it was different at the same time. Solid. Heavy. Strong. With his right hand, he made a fist and struck the concrete next to where he was sitting. A large piece of the concrete step broke off. There was no pain. No effort. The concrete gave so little resistance to his blow. It felt like sticking your hand through a birthday cake. It was easy; it was nothing.

Jack tried to remember all the things the man in the tan jacket said would or might happen to him. Super dense. Hard as a diamond. Probably very heavy, *check on that one,* Jack thought. And, super strong *check on that one too. What was the thing with the rocks sticking to me?* Jack wondered. Even though he was in pain during the transformation, he remembered seeing and feeling the rocks sticking to him. *Was there anything else? Who the hell knows?* he thought as he laid back from the top step onto the cement patio. If he was the only one of his kind, he was just going to have to figure it out on his own. He closed his eyes.

Nine hours later, Jack woke to a dog licking his forehead. He had fallen asleep on the back porch. He had never slept so hard in his life. Standing up, he felt strong. Felt good. Invincible. Jack woke with a singular driving focus. Revenge. It was 5am. Jack's plan was to go to the address the man in the tan jacket gave him. Maybe he could get some answers from them but, he needed a vehicle. He tried his mom's car. The moment he sat down in the driver's seat, the frame bent badly, and made the car undrivable. *That's a problem,* Jack thought. *I'm in Texas, and I have to go to Chicago. I need a vehicle. My motorcycle at the shop! That frame could support my weight. ...but, how to get to the shop? The tractor!* What would normally be an eight minute drive from his house to the shop took thirty minutes on the tractor. The tractor creaked and moaned when he got on it, but it made it there. At five thirty in the morning it was still dark outside. Jack pulled the tractor up around to the side bay door of his shop.

He went to his desk and pulled out a burner phone he kept in his desk drawer. He kept it there in case he needed to send one of his guys on an errand. Jack liked to be able to keep in touch with them. He also pulled some cash out of the safe he kept in his office. Every movement, every motion he made was quick, and precise. He was focused on the task at hand. Get to Chicago. Get information he needed so he could find who killed his family. And, then do right by his mom and little Jimmy, and end them.

Five minutes later, Jack was crouching next to his beefy motorcycle doing some last minute tinkering. Jack heard the door slam from the offices coming into the shop. It was Lou, the older Black gentleman that worked in the shop.

"Hey, Lou. You're in early this morning," said Jack, muffling his stress and anxiety.

"So are you, Mr. Strong," said Lou, as he approached Jack working on his bike.

Jack looked up at Lou, who had a big smile on his face like he was surprised and pleased to see Jack.

"You are here too early. Why would you think you could get in this shop at five in the morning?" asked Jack, in a bit of a skeptical tone. He searched Lou's face for a reaction.

"Jack, I heard about what happened to your family. I'm very sorry," said Lou, ignoring his last line of inquiry.

"Thanks Lou..."

"Do you know why?"

"The sheriff's office is still checking it all out," Jack said. It wasn't the truth, but as the saying went, Jack didn't think Lou could handle the truth.

Lou moved around behind Jack so he could see exactly what Jack was doing.

"Lou, I'm going to be gone for a little while. You'll still answer to Dick for your shop tasks just like always," said Jack, not even looking up at Lou from his focus on the bike.

"But, I would still like an answer to my question, Lou. ...Why would you think someone would be at the shop at five-thirty in the morning?" asked Jack.

There was a loud metallic clang, and Jack felt something hit the back of his head. Jack stood up and saw Lou holding a three-foot long piece of quarter-inch angle iron. He had just struck Jack in the back of the head with it. Of course, the blow had no effect on Jack. His head was now harder and more dense than the carbon steel that had struck him. Jack noticed Lou's face had changed from what it was just a moment before. He no longer had the happy-go-lucky warm smile on his face. He had the same glassy-eyed vacant stare as soldier in the clinic.

"What the hell, Lou?" Jack yelled and stood up to face Lou.

"I see you have taken the catalyst." The words came out of Lou's mouth, but it didn't sound like Lou. The words were slow and measured.

"Lou? Who are you? Who am I speaking to right now? Are you the one that ordered my family to be killed?" Jack asked.

"You are our property, Jack. I know this is alot to take in, but we won't stop until you are either working for us, or you are dead. We made you! Submit yourself to orientation and operation tasking now," said Lou, in a slow menacing voice.

Jack gave a ridiculous chuckle. "You guys just killed my family. There's no way in hell I'm working for you. In fact, I'm going to hunt you down and kill you."

Lou's face smiled a wide, creepy, unnatural smile. "But you will come to work for us, Jack Strong." Lou bent down and picked up an acetylene torch that was in a rig next to Jack and fired it up.

"Lou? What are you doing, Lou?" said Jack, as he slowly got up and held out his hands in an attempt to slow whatever Lou's plans were with the torch.

"If you don't agree to work for us, everyone you know, everyone you love, will die." With that, Lou put the torch to his eye and burnt a hole into his brain. He fell to the ground. Dead.

"No, Lou! Jesus fucking Christ! Good God! What the hell is going on?"

Bending down and putting his right hand on Lou's chest, Jack buried his face in his left hand. He had to think. *How can I stop this from happening?*, he wondered. He rubbed his eyes in disbelief. He just couldn't believe what was happening. His life was going along fine, and then it turned into a carnival of death and destruction. And, other weird stuff, like his density and strength? It was almost like it was happening to someone else. Like he was watching it happening from above. None of it made sense. Sadly, Jack was growing numb to the death that was continuing to happen in his life. His family, his friends, the people at the clinic. All dead. What wasn't numb was the hate he felt for these invisible people. He didn't know who they were. Didn't know where to find them. But, he had a seething hatred for them. Seeing them make Lou kill himself just kicked it up a notch.

Jack didn't even bother calling the sheriff's office to report Lou's body. He got on his bike, fired it up, and left. He figured when the rest of the crew got in they would find it and it would be reported in due course. No need to spend the day answering more of the sheriff's questions. Hell, they might even decide to throw him in jail after Lou's death. Jack didn't need that distraction. He had things to do. People to find. People to kill.

Chapter 9

It had been four and a half hours of straight driving for Jack. He took I-45 into Houston, and then took Highway 59, which headed north, into and through east Texas. Beautiful pine tree county. Jack was always fond of this part of Texas whenever he got to see it, however, on this particular trip he really hadn't even noticed the scenery. His mind was fixed on his objective. Chicago. Meeting the superior of the man in the tan jacket.

Unfortunately, one thing he did notice was that his gas mileage wasn't nearly as good on the bike with him weighing thousands of pounds. He had already stopped once for a fill up. Another thing he noticed was he got hungry much more often. Jack had already consumed three breakfast burritos, and three protein bars he got from his last gas fill up, and was still hungry.

As he continued to drive north on I-59, Jack's mind began to wonder about his condition. It hit him that he knew absolutely nothing about it, this new density. He weighed thousands of pounds. He knew that. His skin seemed to be impenetrable and hard as a diamond. He knew that. He had tremendous strength. He knew that. But, how much strength? What were the limits of his strength? What else could he do that he didn't even know yet? Under normal circumstances, he would take some time and try to find out what he could do. He wanted to know, but there was no time for that. He took a deep breath, and tried to really feel his body as he gripped the handlebars of his massive bike that sped along the highway. His arms. They seemed very heavy, but at the same time he could move them with ease. His entire body felt grounded. He could feel the density, and he could swear that sometimes when he moved his arms and legs in a certain way they made a grinding sound that only he could hear. Not a grinding sound that you would hear at the joints. More like the sound you would hear if you shifted the weight of a bag filled with thousands of tiny ball bearings.

Passing the state line into Arkansas, he was supposed to get on I-30 North ...but he was very hungry. Jack decided to stop on the outskirts of Texarkana to gas up and get something to eat, and he saw a big truck stop up ahead. It was on the same side of the road he was traveling. He liked that. He didn't really want to cross the highway to get gas and eat. *Pain in the ass, and a waste of time,* he thought. The truck stop was big. Trucks filled up on the far left side of the business looking from the road. Cars filled up in front of a large convenience store. There were at least forty gas pumps in all under a very long white and yellow aluminum cover that was positioned in front of the truck stop. There was a small McDonald's attached to the convenience store on the same side the trucks filled up on. On the other side of the store was a more traditional sit down restaurant.

Jack pulled up at a pump to fill up his motorcycle. His body was a little stiff getting off the bike, which creaked with relief when he removed his hefty weight from it's suspension. As he grabbed the gasoline nozzle like he normally would, he noticed he bent the trigger mechanism a little bit. He realized he was going to need to develop a whole other level of sensitivity when he touched and grabbed things. In fact, the only way he recognized he bent the trigger was that he just happened to see it. If he had just been relying upon his touch he never would have known. At this point the little things he was learning about his new body almost moment to moment were becoming less and less surprising ...but, at the same time they fascinated him. While he stood there in front of the pump, Jack reached down in his pocket and made sure he could feel the piece of paper with the address the man in the tan jacket gave him. He rubbed it between his fingers for a moment while recalling that moment just before the strange man died, and handed him the paper with the directive of getting to Chicago. So much blood. So much craziness.

Jack pulled out the burner phone he picked up from his desk earlier that morning, and dialed.

After a few rings a female voice answered "Hello," said Karen.

"Hey, it's me," said Jack, excited to hear her voice.

"Oh my god! I've been so worried about you. Are you ok?"

"Yeah, I'm okay."

"Where are you? Wait! On second thought it's better that you don't say. I heard they found another guy dead in your shop this morning. It's all over the news. They are saying you're a suspect, Jack. They're looking for you."

"Yeah, it happened right in front of me. Poor Lou. These people whoever they are took over his mind ...made him kill himself ...said they wanted me to come and work for them."

"Work?"

"Yeah, but I told them I think I'll just kill them instead." said

"I don't think we should use names when we talk for now, okay? Did you go where I told you to go?" Jack asked.

"Yes."

"Did you bring..."

"Yes," said Karen, cutting Jack off.

"Good. Just stay there until I can get this figured out. These people are dangerous, and I don't know how they are getting in people's heads, but I'm going to figure that out. The more off grid you are the better for now."

"Okay, don't wait too long to call me back. I worry about my guy."

"Your guy worries about you."

"Be careful and don't get killed," said Karen.

"I'm not sure that's even possible anymore. I'm sorry you're in this situation."

"It's not your fault. Now, hang up this phone and go kill those bastards before they hurt anyone else."

Jack parked his motorcycle next to about six other bikes that were parked on the far side of the restaurant. Each of their bikes took a car space by itself. Jack thought that was a ballsy and inconsiderate way to park, because the lot was almost full as it was. By the looks of the bikes, they belonged to a riding club. Harley's mostly.

As he approached the restaurant, he saw a long bar through the windows that ran almost the entire length of the restaurant. It faced the kitchen. Many people were bellied up eating. *Bingo*, Jack thought. He could get some food in him, and eat standing up. He knew he couldn't sit down anywhere. Broken chairs draw attention. *Less attention the better. Eat and go.*

About fifteen minutes, later Jack stood at the far end of the bar, and was about halfway into his eggs, hashbrowns and a pancake. To amuse himself, as he held his fork, Jack was contracting the muscles in his hand and, it wasn't a hard or tight contraction. He was barely contracting the muscles in his hand. Each time he contracted his muscles the salt shaker about three inches away from his hand would slowly move towards him. Then he would replace the salt shaker and do it again. And, again. Jack was mesmerized by it. Couldn't believe it. Didn't understand it. Jack understood that his fist had to be generating a gravitational pull, though. *What else could it be*, he wondered. *There's no magnetism. It has to be gravity.*

Three waitresses were non stop moving to try to keep up with the entire restaurant. A fifty something black waitress behind the bar came by with a half full coffee pot.

"Coffee?"

"Sure, thank you." Jack pushed his empty cup towards her.

As he took a sip, he was taking in the twenty-something fellow that just sat down next to him. Skinny jeans and a backpack. Even though the young man was probably within three years of Jack's age, his immediate impression of him was that he was just a kid. Responsibility matures a person, and Jack had loads of responsibility. Was used to it. Jack expected the young man to be aloof when he sat down, but he gave Jack a big smile and nodded his head to say hello without actually saying hello.

"Is that yours?" The young man pointed to the small Superman action figure Jack had next to his plate.

"Oh, no it was my little brothers. I just had it here... it's my brothers," said Jack, kind of shrugging to say without words that he didn't want to talk about the action figure anymore.

"Superman. The big enchilada. My favorite superhero. I mean, if you're going to be a superhero, why not be Superman, right?"

Jack slowly smiled. "Yeah, I guess so. I think my brother felt... feels the same way." Jack really didn't want to go down the rabbit hole of his brother just dying.

Jack set his fork down on his plate and reached out his hand. "My name is Jack."

"I'm Steve," said the young man.

"I mean unless you run into someone with a pocket full of kryptonite, you are indestructible right? It would be nice to be indestructible."

"You a college student?" Jack asked, trying to change the subject.

"Yes I am. DePaul University."

"You go to college?" Steve asked.

"Me? No, I was going to, but I kinda got side tracked. ...had other obligations. DePaul, huh? You're pretty far away from home."

"Actually, I live near here ...or, my parents do. I was visiting. Headed back to Illinois today," the young man said.

"Gotcha."

"Where are you from?" the young man asked.

"Oh, I'm from Texas. South Texas. I'm just passing through ...stopped to get a bite to eat," Jack replied.

"Where are you headed?" Steve asked.

"I'm headed north. It's not really important. Just going to meet some people," said Jack, not wanting to go into any kind of detail about where exactly or who he was going to meet.

"I'm curious, what's college like? What's a day in college for you?" Jack asked.

"What's it like? Girls, tests, papers, study. I said girls already right?"

Girls? Jack thought, looking at this guy. He didn't seem like he crushes it with the girls.

"Girls? I believe the papers, and the study ...but, you were bullshitting about the girls right?"

Steve studied Jack's face a moment. He was taken aback that Jack would say something so bold to someone he didn't really know.

"Hey, I'm sorry, I just call em like I see 'em. I'm just guessing that you don't crush it with the girls. If I'm wrong, then my bad, and bully for you bud," said Jack, munching on his pancake.

Steve exhaled and looked down a bit. "No, you're right. I don't crush it with girls. Don't get me wrong, I like girls. I can't stop looking at them, but I suck when it comes to talking to them."

"If you want the truth, I was never that great at it either," Jack said.

Steve chuckled. "Yeah right! You look like you would be a total chick magnet."

"What's your field of study?" asked Jack, changing the subject.

"Computer science. I actually have mad hacking skills. I've won a couple of national hacking contests."

"Really? That's a thing?"

"Oh yeah." Steve said, the pride in his accomplishments was apparent.

"Hey you!" said a gruff voice behind Jack and the young man.

Jack turned around and saw a big guy in jeans, boots, and a biker's vest. He had long hair tied into a ponytail. There were three men dressed in similar fashion standing next to him. All of them looked like hardened no-shit guys. Guys you wouldn't normally want to mess with. The biker put his hand on the young man's shoulder and turned him around. He pointed out the window.

"Is that your piece of shit blue Honda Civic out there?"

Steve was clearly scared and intimidated. "Uhhh, yes. It is."

"You bumped my bike when you parked, shit bird."

"I'm sorry, I didn't realize I did."

"Nobody touches my bike." The biker pointed his finger, hitting the young man in the chest, knocking him back against the bar.

"Really, sir. I didn't mean to. It's my bad."

By this time, most of the people in the restaurant were aware something was going on between the bikers and Steve.

"You shut up. I thought about taking it out on your car, but now I think I would rather take it out of your ass." The biker reached out with both hands taking Steve by the shoulders and stood him up.

"All right, that's enough. You guys get back on your bikes and get out of here," said Jack.

The biker let go of Steve and took a quick inventory of Jack, who was still standing between bar stools eating his eggs. Then he looked back at his friends.

"I came in here to whip one guy's ass, but now I guess we get to whip two guys' asses." This statement was met with belly laughs from his friends.

"I don't like bullies," said jack. "And, you are a bully. I'm not going to let you hurt my friend here. Just be smart, and turn around and leave."

"You're not going to 'let' me, huh? I guess I'll start with you then," said the biker as he took a step towards Jack. Jack was a few inches taller than the guy, but that didn't deter the biker.

"I'm asking you again, real nice. Please just get on your bikes and leave, and no one gets hurt," said Jack, in a genuinely respectful manner under the circumstances.

"Come here, you pussy," said the biker.

Jack turned and faced the biker. Normally the biker would have had about forty pounds on Jack. A small panic set in for Jack. Not that he felt the biker could do him any kind of harm, but by this time everyone in the restaurant was watching this unfold. At least a couple already had their phones out ready to record the ensuing ass whipping. Jack didn't need this kind of attention. But, he couldn't just walk away and let them hurt Steve. He liked the kid by now. ...and, besides, it was too late to walk away now. He had already drawn the bikers' attention.

"Are you ready for what's coming?" the biker asked.

Jack chuckled.

"He thinks this is funny," said the biker as he turned around to his friends. Again, met with laughter.

"Let's just skip to the punch line. You wanna hit me? Go ahead. Free shot. I won't move," said Jack calmly.

Without hesitation, the biker reared back and took a swing at Jack, hitting him square in the jaw. The blow, of course, didn't budge Jack. Not even a little bit. The biker immediately dropped to his knees in agony holding his hand. He let out a pathetic howl of pain. The biker looked up at Jack, not understanding what just happened. He couldn't process how hitting Jack felt like hitting a metal statue. The momentum from his blow should have at least caused Jack to move. He didn't move. At all. It just didn't compute for him. He looked at his friend.

"Cut him."

His friend, following orders, pulled out a seven-inch fixed blade knife and held it in Jack's face. He expected Jack to flinch, but Jack just stood there. Jack's thought was if he let these men see they were facing a foe that couldn't be beat, they would leave without anyone getting hurt.

"Go ahead. Cut me." said Jack.

"No dude!" said Steve in a panic.

Jack reached out his hand to Steve as if to say it was okay without saying anything.

The man reared back like he was going to throw a baseball and struck Jack in the base of the neck with the tip of the blade. Again, it was like striking a thick sheet of metal. Jack didn't budge. The biker pulled the blade back and the tip was bent sideways. He looked at Jack like he had seen a ghost.

"What are you, man?" asked the biker with the knife.

Many of the patrons in the restaurant gasped, and there were multiple audible whispers regarding the impossibility of what had just transpired.

"I'm someone you don't want to mess with. Now, get the fuck out of here," said Jack as he pointed towards the door.

No other words were spoken from any of the bikers. They left in a clumsy rush, stealing disbelieving looks at Jack as they made their get-away. Jack looked around and saw at least three people were videotaping with their phones. It pissed him off, but there was nothing he could do about it.

"Nothing to see here folks," said Jack.

Jack reached in his pocket and pulled out some money and placed it next to his plate. He looked at the waitress that had a front row seat for the interaction with the bikers.

"Keep the change," said Jack.

Steve, stood up and faced Jack.

"Thank you, Jack. Those guys were going to tear me a new one. You stopped them."

"Don't mention it. Good luck with your studies." Jack said as he began walking towards the door.

"All that time I really was sitting next to Superman." said the college student.

As Jack walked towards his bike, he could see the bikers had left. He could also see the kids blue Honda Civic was left largely intact by the bikers.

"Excuse me." Jack heard a voice behind him. Turning he could see Steve running towards him.

"You're not going to kill yourself are you?" Jack asked.

"What? No. What?" asked Steve, confused.

"Sorry, I've had a bad couple of days."

"I just wanted to say thanks again. You saved my ass in there." The college student reached out and handed Jack a piece of paper.

"This is my number. If you ever need help with anything, don't hesitate to give me a call. I mean it."

"Thanks." Jack reached out his hand and shook the young man's hand.

"I don't know what you are, but whatever it is it's pretty damn cool," Steve said.

Chapter 10

The events at the restaurant continued to play in Jack's mind as he drove. People videotaped what happened. *Will anyone believe it? No way, they'll think it was doctored,* Jack thought to himself. Still, the attention was unwanted. He also couldn't stop thinking about Lou. *How were they just able to suddenly control him like that? How is that even possible ...and, how many other people do they have their tentacles in? Just average everyday people that he might encounter anywhere?* None of it made sense to Jack. Fortunately, Jack had something to focus on. Something to bring himself back to. *Get to Chicago. Get to the payphone the man in the tan jacket described. Get some answers. Find out who is behind this, and then end it.* End the whole thing with the same violence that they showed his little brother and his mom.

A few hours later, Jack was coming into Memphis, and was already hungry again. His body was feeling stiff, and needed to get up and walk around. Jack decided to stop and get something to eat. As he approached town, he got off Highway 55 onto an adjacent side street. Decided to gas up his bike at a Conoco, and he noticed a little diner down the street. Five minutes later, he was pulling into the place. On top of the diner was a shiny aluminum fifties-style sign with red neon lettering that read *City Diner*. The diner was perfect inside for what Jack needed. As with most diners, it had a bar. He could stand and eat without breaking anything.

It was a cool November day, and the farther north he went, the colder it was getting. It was nice and warm inside the diner. Jack took his jacket off and set it over the chair beside him. The diner was sparsely populated. Jack stood bellied up to the bar drinking a tall glass of iced tea. There was a young couple at a booth on the other end of the diner engaged in what appeared to be a heated conversation. The woman was raising her voice, and the man gave a little panicked look around the restaurant to see if her loud voice was drawing attention. He was imploring her to keep it down.

As he sipped his iced tea, Jack's eyes were drawn to the large windows that faced the street. Across the street was a bus stop with about eight people waiting for a bus. Three were sitting on a bench waiting, and the rest were standing. Jack thought that was a lot of people waiting for a bus this time of day in this neighborhood. Then it escaped his mind as quickly as it entered.

An old man behind the bar sat a big cheeseburger plate in front of Jack. He had made his order a few minutes before. The man had to be in his late sixties. Balding on top.Big gut. White apron on top of a white t-shirt. He behaved in a way that indicated to Jack that he owned the place. There was a contentment to his countenance, and he was very polite to Jack.He was folksy, and friendly and Jack liked that. He had an ease about him that told Jack he didn't have a boss.

"Here you go," he said with a big smile on his face.

"Thank you very much," Jack said.

"It feels nice and warm in here. It's pretty cool outside." He felt a small obligation to make conversation, considering he and the old man were really the only ones on that side of the diner.

"Density," said the old man.

Jack stopped chewing and looked up at the old man that had just been smiling at him a moment before. The old man's face was no longer smiling. It had the glassy eyed, non blinking stare he had come to recognize as being under the influence of someone else.

"Excuse me?"

"Density. That is what I called the program that made you," said the old man.

"Who am I speaking with?" said Jack.

"I am General Max Mellig. I made you. You could say I am your father in a way."

"General? Have we spoken before?"

"No, you spoke to others previously."

"Why did you kill my family?"

"They were casualties of war, I'm afraid. A needless distraction for you."

"I'm going to kill you, you know," said Jack.

"Are you now?" said the old man as a strange, creepy smile stretched across his face.

"You know, Jack. You will learn ...you will learn your place. You will learn I'm not one to be trifled with. You are under the impression that you are operating independently of me, but I control everything. You will be just another cog in my wheel of control. ...but what a cog!"

"Hey..." Jack said. The old man stopped talking for a moment.

"What ever kind of pontificating threatening bullshit you are about to say to me, you can just shut the fuck up. I'm not interested," said Jack.

Mellig continued to speak through the old man, ignoring Jack's words.

"I had to speak with you personally, Jack. I have so many questions for you. After all these years, I had to see you. To see the fruits of my labor. I have to know things about you. Such as... what are the limits of your density? How has it affected your strength?"

"Piss off. I'm eating," said Jack without looking up from his burger.

The old man chuckled. "You have your mother's same feisty attitude."

"You knew my real mother?" Jack said as he put his hamburger down on the plate.

"Of course I knew her. She was the lab assistant aiding the doctor when the accident occurred. That's how she became infected with the density agent, and in turn, how you became infected with it. Unfortunately, she didn't survive your birth. But, you sure did."

"She's dead? Did you know my real father?"

"Yes, I did. I can answer all the questions you no doubt have about your real parents, Jack. All you have to do is submit yourself for active-duty service to us."

"You seem to control everyone else. Why can't you just flip a switch and control me like you're doing now to this poor old man?" said Jack, motioning towards the old man with a French fry in his hand.

The old man belted out an eerie laugh.

"You don't get answers to questions like that. Enough talking. I'm going to start finding answers to my questions."

"I'm not giving you any answers."

"Oh, yes you will. Look across the street. You see those people waiting for the bus? In about forty-five seconds they will be run over by a city bus going in excess of fifty miles an hour. They will all die ...unless you save them, Jack."

Jack turned around and looked at the bus stop. There were more people waiting for the bus now than when he came into the restaurant. At least ten. He put his cheeseburger down and began to walk towards the door. Mainly he just wanted to see if Mellig was bullshitting him.

"Hey, where ya goin'?" said the old man from behind him.

Jack turned and could immediately tell the old man was no longer under the influence of the General.

"I'll be right back," said Jack.

Jack walked outside and looked both ways down the street. Sure enough, to his right was a city bus coming fast. He crossed the street on a line towards the group waiting at the bus stop.

"Hey!" Jack belted out loudly.

They all looked up at him.

"You're all about to die unless you get back behind the corner of that building." Jack pointed at a small commercial storefront about twenty feet behind them.

The people looked at each other for a moment, but didn't move.

"I mean it! Get up and leave this area!"

Finally, one older lady carrying a large handbag got up and walked towards the side of the building. Then four others followed. The rest stayed put. The ones that stayed put had the glassy eyed dull gaze. One of them, an older Black man, spoke to Jack.

"They're not going to get up, Jack."

Jack looked down the street. The bus was coming, and it was coming fast.

"Jesus!" Jack said to himself with a note of wavering commitment for what he must do.

He thought quickly. If he just stopped the bus cold he would save the people at the bus stop, but probably injure many on the bus. He needed to keep the bus from hitting the bus stop, but stop it slowly to keep from injuring those inside. What happened next was complete intuition. The bus was coming up on the end of the block about two football fields away. Jack had never once tried to jump since Karen injected him with the catalyst, and he made the genetic change into what Mellig called "Density." And yet, he knew like he knew his own name that when he did, he could jump very, very far. He knew it because he could feel the strength in his legs, his quadriceps, his glutes. He knew they would catapult him like a rail gun. Jack bent down and then jumped. Just as he anticipated, he shot into the air like he was shot out of a cannon. To Jack it felt like he was in the air for minutes, but it was actually just a few seconds. He kept moving his arms back and forth to balance himself so he would land on his feet.

Finally, Jack landed about half way down the block in the middle of the street, feet first, with a loud crashing sound. His feet went ankle deep into the pavement. He stepped out of the hole he created and waited for the bus to reach him. It didn't take long. The bus had to be traveling about forty-five to fifty miles an hour. Seconds before the bus reached him he could see the driver. Glassy-eyed, dull stare with a crazy wide smile. Then came the collision. Jack latched onto the front of the bus. His hands dug into the metal just beneath the front windshield so he would have something to hold on to. The grill and front of the bus were constructed of pressed aluminum and steel. It all felt like aluminum foil to Jack. His fingers mashed into it and bent it with ease. He started running backward with the bus. Each time he put a foot down, he crashed it three inches deep into the pavement. And with each step, the bus slowed a bit. Thirty miles an hour, twenty, ten, and finally it came to a stop about thirty feet in front of the bus stop.

Even though the bus was stopped, the wheels were still smoking. The driver still had his foot on the gas. With his right hand, Jack punched into the engine compartment. He couldn't really see through the grill, but he just started ripping apart whatever his hand fell on. The third time was the charm. Whatever he ripped that time did the trick and the engine gave a sputter, and then stopped. Jack looked up at the driver, who still had the wide glassy eyed stare and crazy smile. He was staring down at Jack. Taking a step back from the front of the bus, Jack stared at the driver. He flipped him the bird, knowing it was really the general or one of his minions he was flipping off, and then proceeded to walk back into the diner. The occupants of the diner clearly had just witnessed Jack just stop a twenty-ton bus. They stared at him like they didn't know what to make of him. Fearful stares. The couple that was arguing previously were up out of their booth, and taking steps backward to put space in between Jack and them. The old bald man still stood at the window, mouth open, gaping at the bus.

"You just stopped that bus!" said the old bald man that Mellig had previously used to speak through.

"Yes, I did."

"But how? No one can do that. How?" said the old man, pointing at the bus.

"I drank a lot of milk as a boy. It's good for your bones."

Jack pointed at his hamburger. "Gotta finish my lunch." Jack bellied back up to his half-eaten burger.

The bald man approached Jack. "What are you going to do now?"

"I'm going to finish my lunch," said Jack, as he stuffed some fries in his mouth.

"These are good fries!" said Jack. "...did you make these?"

The bald man looked at the fries and then back to Jack. He nodded his head without saying anything.

"I didn't catch your name," Jack said.

"Uh, it's Al," said the old man, still in the kind of shock you fall into when you see something that changes your understanding of how the world works. Of what's possible.

"Well Al, those are the best fries I've had in at least six months ...maybe eight. For real. Good job," said Jack, as he got up and wiped his mouth on a napkin. Grabbing what was left of his burger, Jack began to walk towards the door, patting Al on the back as he passed him.

"Have a good day, Al."

Chapter 11

It was all Jack could do to put on a brave face for Al at the diner. He was shaken to his core. It's hard to fight an enemy you can't see, but one that can jump from person to person? *How is he controlling these people? What the hell is going on? And, then to just switch it on and off at will. How?* Jack's thoughts raced through his mind. *And, then how did he know I was at the diner? How did he know when to switch on the bald guy and talk to me? Can he see through their eyes even when he's not controlling them?* None of it made any sense to Jack, and it frightened him to think about the lack of control he had over the whole thing. *He doesn't seem to control everyone, but he controls a lot of people.* Jack thought since he couldn't tell the difference between the ones the general could control and those he couldn't, that it would be safe and smart to assume that the general controls everyone. Keep a low profile. Head down …not that they could hurt him, but he really didn't want the general to know where he was headed.

Before he got back on the highway, Jack stopped at a truck stop. He parked around the back of the store, so no one could see him get off his bike. Inside he bought a grey hoodie,, and some sunglasses. Once outside, he put the hoodie on over his leather jacket with the top pulled down over his head, then put on his helmet. He wished he could do something to conceal his bike, but they didn't sell hoodie's for bikes.

It normally took around eight hours to drive from Memphis to Chicago. Jack made it in six hours and fifty-two minutes. Once he entered Chicago, it took Jack another thirty-five minutes to navigate to the address the man in the tan jacket gave him. Wasn't in the best of neighborhoods. He gave Jack an address on S. Damen Ave on the southside of Chicago. It was dirty. Graffiti on most of the buildings. For the first time he could remember, Jack was suddenly aware that he was a white guy in a Black neighborhood. He was getting a lot of "Who are you?" and "You don't belong here" stares from the occupants. Approaching the address, Jack slowed way down. The address led him to a convenience store that occupied the ground floor of an old red brick building. Jack took it all in. It was on the corner with the door opening towards the apex of the corner. It was dirty. Not just dirty, but the kind of dirty that's been there a while ...like decades. Jack thought it smelled like stale beer. As he turned the corner in front of the store, he saw the pay phone. It sat just behind a blue US mailbox, tucked up against the red brick of the building.

Jack's eyes zeroed in on the phone. The cord was still there, as well as the handset. *Who uses a pay phone anymore anyway?* Jack thought to himself. When Jack reached the end of the store, he did a slow U-turn in the street and parked his bike next to the curb in front of a building on the opposite side of the street facing the pay phone. It was a one-story brick building. The brick was lighter and more orange than the convenience store. The windows had those little glass bricks in them instead of glass panes, the kind of glass bricks you can't see through. It appeared to be abandoned, no one was around, the doors were closed with no signs around them, and it was dark inside. Before getting off his bike, Jack slowly scanned the area. Behind him a neighborhood began, if it could be called a neighborhood. Looked like every other home was abandoned. Couches in front yards. The homes themselves were in poor condition. Not a lot of tender love and care. Jack heard a baby crying.

On the opposite corner of the store was a dirty dive bar. The neon light above the door spelled out BAR. The lack of imagination on the name of the bar amused Jack. In front of the bar, on the corner, were three Black men. Looked to be in their early twenties. They were laughing amongst themselves, but were also acutely aware of Jack's presence. Jack needed to make the phone call ...but first things first. Jack walked across the street and entered the store. The three young Black men watched. Jack still had his hoodie on. Still had it pulled up tight over his head. Couldn't see his face unless he was looking right at you.

Approximately three minutes later, Jack emerged from the store with a bag containing three sandwiches wrapped in plastic and a bottle of water ...well, two actually. He was already munching on one of the sandwiches. It occurred to Jack that he had felt hungry all day long, and it's not like he hadn't been eating. He ate. A lot. But inevitably, soon after eating he was hungry again.

Jack walked down to the pay phone. He picked it up and held it to his ear with his shoulder. Without removing the sandwich from his hand, he poked out his index finger and dialed three sevens. There were three clicks. And, then after about five seconds, a female voice came on the phone. She said, "Stay there. We are sending someone to get you," and then the line went dead. Jack hung up the phone and walked back towards where his bike was parked. There was a bench bolted to the ground up against the orange brick building. Jack knew what would happen if he sat on the bench, so instead, he sat on the tall curb next to his bike, and continued to eat his sandwich.

Jack felt a small sense of relief. *It's about goddamn time,* he thought. *Maybe now I'll start to get some answers.* Without looking Jack could hear the three young Black men approaching him from behind. It wasn't long before they were standing directly behind him.

"Yo muther fucker, you jus' parked your big ass bike in the wrong neighborhood. Now give me yo' money."

Still chewing his sandwich, Jack slowly turned to see who was speaking to him. It was the tallest of the three men. He had a dirty white wife beater t-shirt on, and blue jeans that were barely hanging onto his ass. He had a pistol pointed at Jack's head.

"Come on muther fucker! I ain't fucking around!" said the angry young man.

Jack turned his back again to the young man and continued to eat his sandwich.

"Sig Saur P-238. That's kind of a girly gun for a dude. I mean, seriously? A three eighty is kind of a woman's round, don't ya think?" said Jack, in a calm, humorous tone.

"How you know what kind of rounds I got, man?" said the tall, angry Black man.

"I'm from Texas," said Jack without turning around.

"Texas?" asked the Black man as he looked at the shorter youth next to him. The shorter guy just shrugged his shoulders.

"Okay, Okay ...don't matter what rounds I got man! They'll still kill "yo' ass!"

"Yo, B-Ball, plug his ass right now! He's talking shit to you!" said one of the other young Black men to the tall one in the white t-shirt.

"B-Ball? What kind of a name is B-Ball?" said Jack, with a chuckle. "I'm just saying, man if I were a dude I would be embarrassed to carry that gun around."

"Fuck you man!" shouted B-Ball. Then he pulled the trigger. Bang! The gunshot reverberated in Jack's skull. The bullet bounced off the back of Jack's head and splintered part of the wood on the bench behind where the young thugs were now standing.

Jack didn't turn around. He took another bite of his sandwich. "I told you it was a woman's gun, B-Ball. Not even strong enough to break my skin... pathetic," said Jack, somewhat amused with himself.

B-Ball looked at his gun. He and his boys couldn't quite process what they had just seen. They were alternating staring at the gun, Jack, and each other in no particular order.

"Yo man, why ain't you dead?" asked B-Ball.

"Maybe it was just a dud bullet. Why don't you shoot me again?" said Jack, while munching on his sandwich, head still facing away from the thugs behind him.

"B-Ball, I don't like this man. There's something not right with this dude," said one of B-Ball's fellow thugs.

B-Ball fired three more rounds into the back of Jack's head. Loud, loud, loud. Tore the hell out of the back of Jack's hoodie. Bullets ricocheting everywhere. B-Ball's friends were running for cover.

Jack reached into his bag and took out another sandwich and began to unwrap it.

"Don't let it get you down, B-Ball. Even punk ass thug murderers like yourself have bad days . You'll be murdering again in no time. Keep your chin up," said Jack.

Suddenly, a large black suburban swung around the corner and parked in front of the payphone, but in the middle of the street. Three men got out, two in black tactical gear. Each holding an AR-15 strapped to his shoulder. Muzzles pointed at the ground. The other man had a black suit and a black tie over a white shirt. Jack didn't get up from where he was sitting. He continued to eat his sandwich. The three thugs each took a couple of steps back.

The two men in tactical gear quickly scanned up and down the street. One of them said to the man in the suit "I don't see him anywhere."

The man in the suit looked over at Jack. "Who dialed that phone?"

"I did," said Jack as he was finishing up the last bite of the last sandwich. Jack wadded up the bag he got from the store and tossed it into a green metal trash can close to his bike. Jack then stood up and took a couple of steps towards the man in the suit. The two men with AR's both raised their muzzles and pointed them towards Jack.

"That's close enough." one of them said.

"Who are you?" asked the man in the suit.

"My name is Jack Strong."

"Where's Agent Crawford?" inquired the man in the suit.

"Who? Oh, you mean the man that gave me your info?"

"Yes, that man."

"Yeah, he's dead. Killed by a nurse. Shot him in the back," said Jack.

"Did he give you a syringe before he died?"

"Yes he did."

"Where is it? I'll need that back right now," said the man in the suit with an angry tone.

"I had to inject it. Actually, my friend injected it. Because I was almost dead ...saved my life."

"So, your..." The agent shot a quick look at the two men in tactical gear.

Jack cut the guy off. "No, I'm going to ask the questions. Who the fuck are you guys? My whole family has been murdered and I need answers to a lot of questions."

"We've got some answers, but first we need to make sure you are who you say you are," said the suited agent sternly.

Jack turned around and looked at B-Ball. "B-Ball, you need to wear a belt with those jeans. They are falling off your ass."

B-Ball instantly developed an angry sneer across his face, raised his pistol, and shot Jack square in the chest. The bullet ricocheted off his chest and broke one of the small glass blocks in the building behind his bike.

Jack turned and faced the suited agent, and raised his shirt. "No vest. I'm the guy you're looking for."

"Alright, get in the vehicle," said the suited agent.

"No, that's not going to work for me. One, I'm not leaving my bike in this shit hole neighborhood. And, two I'm pretty sure I would ruin your vehicle if I tried to get in it. I'll follow you," said Jack, as he swung his leg over his bike and fired it up.

The man with the suit walked over to Jack and took a little black device out of his pocket. The device was no bigger than a credit card. He held it near the back of Jack's head for a brief moment, and then he took a quick look at it.

"He's clear," said the man in the suit to the two men in tactical gear.

Before Jack took off, he looked over at B-Ball.

"What are you man?" B-Ball asked.

"God sent me. Killing people for money? You already punched your ticket to hell. But, if you stop right now and start helping people instead of hurting them, you might have a chance to get into heaven...maybe. Nah, on second thought, you are going to hell B-Ball. Definitely going to hell. Tell Satan to fuck off for me."

Chapter 12

Jack followed behind their Tahoe for around three miles. They pulled into a long alley way in between two red brick warehouses that looked to be abandoned on S. Western Boulevard. It was an industrial area, a mixture of warehouses, factories, and vacant lots. At least half the buildings looked like they hadn't been occupied in years. The buildings were two stories and old. There was a white molded stone bevel in between the two stories that was covered in dark dirty soot. Could barely see the white in some places. There were large slate windows that appeared to open several window panels at one time along the facade that faced the street. However, they were dark and dirty, and looked like they hadn't been opened in a long time. There was only darkness beyond the frosted glass of the windows. No light shining from within the building. No sign of life anywhere.

At the far end of the alley, there was a bay door in the building on the left. Jack could see the door was in the process of opening as they were driving up. There was about a fifteen-foot tree fighting to grow in a large crack in the ground just a little farther down the alley. Looked like the tree used to be a weed, and no one ever cut it down. .The SUV pulled inside the building. Jack parked his bike in the alley a little ways down from the door. He dismounted his bike and walked through the large open door after the Tahoe. The warehouse was largely empty. The man in the tie pulled the Tahoe up about forty feet in front of the bay door and slightly to the left. Parked. One of the men in tactical gear got out of the Tahoe and walked to the bay door. He looked down the alley they just traveled down. Poked his head back inside, and pushed a button to shut the large door.

The warehouse was dimly lit. About a football field long. Jack stood with his back to the bay door taking in the warehouse. There was a long empty table pushed up against the wall to his right. At the far end of the warehouse to the left against the wall were four large wooden crates. And, in the center of the far wall was an entrance to a freight elevator. Other than that, the entire warehouse was just one large empty space.

The man in the tie looked at Jack. "Follow me," he said, as he walked towards the freight elevator. As soon as the door closed on the elevator, Jack could feel it started to go down. Judging by the shortness of the trip, Jack figured they couldn't have been more than one or two stories underground. The door opened, and Jack followed the three men out of the elevator. The scene reminded Jack of the resistance headquarters from *Star Wars*. Busy people. Moving with purpose to fight a common enemy. To the right was a two story glass office space from floor to ceiling. The glass offices were built up against the side of the warehouse space. Jack could see people working through the glass on both floors. Some glanced up and looked to see who was coming out of the elevator. Towards the end of the glass office space, on the bottom floor, there were men and women in lab coats working in what appeared to be a laboratory. To the left of Jack was a large curved desk against the wall with an attractive woman in uniform sitting behind the desk on the phone.

Walking ahead of Jack, the man in the black tie whispered something to the two men in tactical gear, and they quickly changed their course to the right, disappearing around a corner in front of the glass offices. In the center of the warehouse space was a long footprint of single story offices, about thirty-five feet wide, and a couple of hundred feet long. No windows in these offices. Just off white walls, and doors. The man in the black tie led Jack down a long hallway on the left side of the middle footprint of offices. Jack thought it looked like a maze you would send a mouse into looking for cheese. About two-thirds of the way down the man in the black tie stopped and opened a door on the right. He stepped aside as if to allow Jack to enter.

"You're not coming in?" asked Jack quietly.

"No," said the man in the black tie. He motioned with his hand towards the door.

Jack walked through the door, and the man in the black tie shut the door behind him. Jack found himself standing in a large conference room. No windows. In the center of the room there was black conference table about twenty feet long. There were ten people seated around the table, and another five or six standing down near the far end of the table. There were four men dressed in military officer gear seated at the table, including one at the head of the table. The rest were dressed in professional attire, except one wore a white lab coat. Three were women. Jack also noticed one of the people standing near the end of the table was the Speaker of the House of Representatives. All of their eyes were firmly fixed on Jack. The silver haired officer seated at the end of the table stood up and faced Jack.

"Welcome Jack, we are excited to meet you. My name is Colonel David Tolbert."

Jack nodded in his direction, but said nothing.

A woman in a dark pantsuit standing near the Speaker of the House spoke up in a shrill stilted tone. "Before you say another word to him we need to know he is for real, and double check for tagging." The woman turned her head towards the man in the white lab coat. The man in the coat took the woman's stare as instructions to examine Jack. He awkwardly approached Jack, reached in his pocket and took out a small black card. The same kind of card the men dressed in tactical gear waved behind his head previously. The man in the coat reached behind Jack's head with the card and a green light showed clearly on the card. The man in the coat held up the card for all the room to see.

Jack pushed the man back with one hand. "Just a sec bud." Jack looked at Colonel David Tolbert and said, "I don't know who you guys are, or what this is, but I just want to know two things. What is it exactly that I'm dealing with here, and the location of the guy that ordered my family to be killed. I'll do the rest."

"All your questions will be answered, Jack. We want to know about you as much as you want to know about us. Please let the man finish," said Colonel Tolbert.

The lab tech in the white coat motioned for Jack to step atop what looked like a large black industrial scale about three inches off the ground. Four feet by six feet, with a weight display on one end. Jack stepped atop the scale. The scale screeched in a high pitch. The man in the lap coat read the display allowed for all to hear...

"Ten thousand four hundred and seventy-two pounds." Then he wrote the number down on his clipboard.

"My poor bike," Jack muttered to himself under his breath as he stepped off the scale.

There were hushed whispers among the occupants of the room. Then the man in the white lab coat walked over to a case sitting on a nearby table. He pulled out a rather large hypodermic needle. "I need to take some blood from you, Mr. Strong."

"That's not really going to work out for you, I'm afraid," said Jack.

"What? Why not?" asked the man in the lab coat.

"Let's just save us all some time shall we?" Jack said. "Colonel Tolbert, would you mind shooting me in the head with your firearm please?"

"Trust me." said Jack, as he noticed hesitation on the colonel's face.

Colonel Talbot walked over, and stood facing Jack. He pulled out his firearm, and held it approximately a foot away from Jack's head and pulled the trigger. The blast from the gun was very loud in the enclosed room. It shocked everyone a little bit, in spite of them holding their hands over their ears.

Jack stood there smiling at the colonel. Unharmed. "I'm still not used to it either."

"Now, what the hell am I? Who is this General Max Mellig? How is he able to control certain people? And how can I find him?"

The colonel lowered his gun and began to speak to Jack.

"Twenty-five years ago Max Mellig was put in charge of a research and development project called Density. He was a colonel at that time. It was actually his brainchild. He lobbied for it. He was, and still is, obsessed with creating the perfect killing weapon.

"Your mother was a scientist and assisted the doctor in charge of the Density Project. Your mother was pregnant with you when there was an accident in the lab. The accident killed the doctor in charge, and inadvertently infected you with the Density gene in vitro.

"After the accident, Mellig lost his funding for the Density Project. After all, the doctor that developed it was now dead. You, Jack, are the one and only successful outcome of the Density Project."

"You know my mother?" Jack asked.

"No, I never knew her personally. I'm just familiar with the facts," said Colonel Tolbert.

"Go on..."

"Your mother is dead, Jack. I'm sorry to tell you that. She died giving birth to you. Before you were six weeks old, you were taken from Mellig. Kidnapped, as it were."

"By who?"

"By a gentleman named Sebastian Coe. At the time, he was a scientist that worked for Mellig. He was also your grandfather."

"What? My grandfather?" Jack asked, with a note of excitement.

"Yes, he knew what kind of life was in store for you in Mellig's care, so he organized a snatch, and placed you with the family you grew up with. He was the only one who knew your location."

"Is my grandfather still alive?"

"I don't know."

The woman in the dark pantsuit interrupted. "This is ridiculous! Even with his abilities, what can one man do against Mellig's machine? This is fool's gold."

After a brief silence, Jack spoke up. "She's right. You shouldn't put your faith in me. ...besides, I'm not here for you. I'm here for me. I'm going to kill the bastard that killed my family. Your cause takes a back seat to mine."

"Fortunately, your cause and ours share the same outcome," said the Speaker of the House of Representatives. "Mellig must be stopped."

"How does he control people?" asked Jack.

Colonel Tolbert spoke up. "After the Density project failed Mellig went on to start many covert projects. Most were failures, but there were some successes. He had a fabricated soldier project that was a success ...robots, if you will. Robots that kill. But, his most spectacular success was his cortex chip project."

"Cortex chip?"

"Yes, he had a tiny chip developed, that when inserted into the cerebellum it has the ability to take control of a human being. He can see what the person with the chip sees. He can speak through the person, and he can get them to do whatever he wants. And, when he flips the switch back, the person is completely unaware they carry the chip."

"That's what the card is that you place behind people's heads ...to see if they carry the chip?" Jack asked, putting two and two together.

"Exactly. Unfortunately, it's way worse than you can imagine. He has tagged the president, the entire cabinet, most of congress, most world leaders. And now, he's going for everyone. For all intents and purposes he controls what goes on in our world. You are looking at some of the very few people in positions of power that haven't been inserted."

"So, people just let him put this chip in?"

"He's been using the medical community. Most all medical doctors and technicians in medium to large cities are all chipped. And when people come in for medical check ups or procedures they in turn get chipped. The thing is, the chip is inserted with a small needle. Doesn't require surgery, so it's fast and easy for them. Everyone eventually goes to the doctor. That's when they get people. Slowly but surely they are making their way into smaller towns. And, with some important targets, he sends teams in to kidnap them and chip them."

"That's how he got people to go along with this blood program for young men? The Watson Act?" Jack asked.

"Yes, he implemented that program to find you, Jack. That's the only purpose for it."

"Why did he want me so bad?"

"He wanted to catch you before you had taken the catalyst. If you can control someone with immense strength that can't be killed, that's quite a weapon. Now he wants you for another reason. Since you have already taken the catalyst, he can no longer insert the chip in you. You are too dense. You are the one person on the planet that he can't control, and he can't destroy you. You represent a big danger to him."

"You are wrong. He didn't want to catch me. He wanted to kill me. He sent someone to my home. He killed my family, and he tried to kill me, but I killed his hit-man before he finished me off," said Jack through gritted teeth.

The female with the dark pantsuit spoke directly to Jack. "You say he killed your entire family? Is there no one left that's important to you?"

"Yes, there is, but I sent her away to her family's cabin. She's safe."

"No, she's not safe," said the woman in the dark pantsuit. "She's either dead, or she's been implanted with a chip by now. Mellig doesn't leave stones like that unturned, and he will use her to control you. ...believe me!"

A bolt of nervous anxiety went up Jack's spine hearing that Karen might be dead. "Look, I just need to know where to find this guy. Where is Mellig?" said Jack, as he walked over to a box sitting on a table in front of the man with the lab coat that weighed him. The box had several of these small cards used to see if people had been implanted with a chip. Jack reached in and took out three of them, put them in his pocket, and started to walk back to where he was standing nearer the door.

The man in the white coat grabbed Jack by the arm. "Hey you can't take those! They don't belong to you!"

Jack whipped around, looked down at the man's hand on his arm, and then into the man's face. "I'm taking them."

The man in the coat stopped in his tracks. Jack continued to walk away from him. "Now someone tell me where Mellig is please."

"We don't know where he is," said Colonel Tolbert.

Chapter 13

"Take him to the twins. We need to know as much about Jack and what he can do as possible," Colonel Tolbert said to the man in the black-tie that had met Jack by the convenience store and brought him in previously. The meeting in the conference room had just concluded a few moments before, and Jack had finally calmed down a little. He was excited to be learning the details of his enemy, and that there were people that could help him.

The man in the black tie looked at Jack. "Follow me," he said, as he began walking down the hall. Jack followed.

"The twins?" asked Jack.

"You'll see."

They went back through the lobby, and all the way around to the other side of the building where Jack had previously seen the glass windowed walls of people wearing lab coats working in what looked like a lab. Sure enough it was a lab. The man in the black tie stopped at the door to the lab and opened it up for Jack.

"You're not going in?" Jack asked, looking at him.

The man in the black tie shook his head no.

Jack stepped through the door to the lab, and had to adjust his eyes a little bit because everything was a very bright white. The floors were a white tile. There were three long tables that ran most of the width of the lab that bisected the lab at equal distances apart. White cabinets under the tables. However, the top of the tables were covered in a slick black shiny surface. White storage cabinets along the far wall opposite the windows. And, of course white ceiling tiles. The room was brightly lit with several large four-foot fluorescent lights hanging down from the high ceilings.

Two women approached Jack, both in white lab coats, worn over grey pants and white button down shirts underneath. Every aspect of their clothing was identical. They both had sandy blond hair that fell just to their shoulders. Both had a big smile on their faces. He estimated they were in their early thirties. Jack thought they were attractive in a nerdy sort of way.

"Look, Abbie, it's a man!"

"A man indeed, Annie!"

"Hello," said Jack, giving a little waist level half-wave, and a half smile.

"Let me guess... you guys are twins," Jack said.

"I just met her two days ago," said Annie pointing at Abbie. "People say we look alike, but I'm not seeing it."

Abbie looked at Jack and gave a sort of pig snort. "That was a joke. Annie, tell the man you were joking."

"I was joking," said Annie, also giving a little bit of a snort laugh.

Annie... Abbie... Jack didn't know who was who. Didn't really care, even though he liked the whimsical nature of the girls. He decided to just not use their names when speaking to them.

"The colonel told us two days ago we might be getting to examine you, after he got word from our operative that was assigned to you. How is he by the way? Abbie had a thing for him," said Annie.

"He's dead." Jack said matter-of -factly.

"Okay. Bad news, Abbie. You'll have to restart your elaborate fantasy fixation with a new subject," said Annie while looking at Abbie in a rather callous way.

"He was a good man. Go shave your gorilla underarms," said Abbie to her sister.

"...Ladies, why don't we just get down to business," Jack said.

"He's right," said Abbie.

"We've been told you have already taken the catalyst, and that you weigh over ten thousand four hundred pounds. Is that correct?" said Annie, addressing Jack. She was writing on a clipboard.

"Yes, that's correct."

"We have speculated that your skin has developed a hardness. We would like to test that if you don't mind," said Annie. She looked up from her clipboard and pointed across the room. "Abbie would you mind getting the Mohs stick for me?"

"Mohs stick?" Jack asked.

"The Mohs scale of hardness was developed by a guy with the last name of Moh," said Annie.

"Go figure," said Abbie, as she handed her the curved metal apparatus.

"Anyway, it was designed as a simple way to test the hardness of rocks and minerals. If you scratch one type of mineral with another type of mineral, and one of them makes a scratch on the other one then the one that did the scratching is harder than the one that got scratched. At the top of that scale of hardness are Abbie's nipples when it's cold in here. However, just slightly below that is the diamond ...and we have a diamond attached to the end of this little stick that I'm about to scratch you with."

Jack looked at Abbie and smiled.

"She's a kidder," Abbie said with a deadpan face.

Annie took the stick, reached over, and gave Jack a good swipe across his arm. There was a small billow of faint white dust that came as a result of the swipe. Jacked looked down and brushed the dust off his arm, revealing no damage at all to his skin. Annie then pulled the end of the stick close to her eyes, and examined the diamond.

"I'll be ...I think you took the tip off my diamond."

"Did it scratch your arm?" Annie asked.

"No," said Jack, looking down at his arm.

"And, what does that mean?" Annie again asked.

"It means my arm is harder than the diamond," Jack said with a little question inflection at the end.

"Abbie, remind me to give him a sucker when we are done. That's correct, your skin is harder than a diamond. I'll spare you the agony of scratching you with Abbie's nipples."

"He would love it!" Abbie said, shooting Jack a little wink and a smile.

Annie finished writing on her clipboard, and set it down. "Okay, so we have the weight, and the hardness of the skin ...what else? What else has changed with you since you have taken the catalyst?" Annie asked.

"I'm stronger than I used to be. A lot stronger," Jack said.

Annie clapped her hands. "Okay, strength. I'm not going to test every muscle group. Let's just test your press and see where that gets us."

"You mean bench press?" Jack asked.

"Yes, your bench press," said Annie. She started walking towards the end of the laboratory. Jack could see a large hydraulic press against the wall.

"Brought this big mamma jamma in just for you!" said Abbie, walking behind Jack.

The press was big and green. Except there were two stainless steel cylinders that led down to a green flat piece of metal about three inches thick, twenty inches wide and four feet long. Underneath this was a metal table or platform supported by a lot of steel underneath.

"Jack, get up there on that table and lay down for me, if you would, with your shoulders under the press."

Jack obliged. Reminded him of being inside a ct scan machine, except this one could crush your skull. Looking over at Annie, Jack gave a little thumbs up.

"We're going to start you off at three hundred pounds, okay?" Abbie said with her hand on the switch.

Jack nodded without saying anything. He placed his hands flat on the press in front of his face. Abbie flipped the switch. You could hear the hum of the hydraulics, but there was no movement. Jack held it in place.

"Let me save us some time. Why don't you start off at five thousand pounds." Jack said.

The twin sisters looked at each other. Annie nodded at Abbie, and Abbie set the calibration to five thousand pounds.

"Okay, but if your head gets squished, I can't promise what Abbie will do with the rest of your body," Annie said.

"Trim your nose hair," Abbie said to her sister. "You ready?" Abbie said to Jack.

Jack nodded his head. Abbie flipped the switch. The hum was louder from the machine this time, but the machine didn't budge. Jack was holding it firm.

"Okay, that felt like nothing ...let's bump it in increments of ten thousand," Jack said.

"Your wish is my command," Abbie said. Annie was busy writing on the clipboard.

Seven minutes later, the weight was at one hundred thousand pounds. The twins were dumbfounded. There were at least five or six people observing from the glass outside the lab.

"Okay, Jack we are at fifty tons. This machine only goes up to eighty tons. How did that last one feel?" Annie said.

Jack had a smile on his face, because this is something he'd been wanting to do. He wanted to know the limits of his capabilities.

"It's weird, I can feel that it's heavy, but my body just responds to the weight ...almost like it has a mind of its own," said Jack. "Just put it at eighty tons and let's see what happens."

Abbie looked at Annie, her eyes growing wider. Annie nodded. Abbie reset the calibration.

"You ready?" Abbie asked.

Jack nodded. She flipped the switch. The machine made its first progress downward toward Jack's head. One inch. Two inches ...and, then it stopped. Jack's face was red, and his head was shaking a little from the strain. Then, the press started to go back up. Finally Jack's arms extended all the way up, and something broke in the machine. It made a loud popping noise, like an engine throwing a rod. Abbie quickly reached over and unplugged the machine from the wall.

Annie made a note on her clipboard, and finished it with a flamboyant swoosh with her pen. "Okay, eighty tons. Check! .Abbie do you realize what this means?"

"That his erection could penetrate a brick wall?" Abbie asked.

"I was going to say concrete ...but I like where your heads at!" Annie said, as she gave her sister a high five.

"Okay, Jack. You weigh a ton ...well, five tons actually. Your skin is harder than a diamond, and you can lift eighty tons. What else? What else can you do?" Annie said, with her hands on her hips.

Jack stepped down from the metal platform that was part of the hydraulic press. "Um... let's see. I can jump really high, but that kinda goes with strength. Oh! There's the gravity thing!"

"Gravity? What do you mean?" Annie asked.

"Well, I'm not quite sure what it is, but if I had to say, I would say my body can generate its own gravitational field, but only when I contract my muscles in a certain way," Jack said.

"Here, I'll show you. May I borrow your pen?" He held out his hand to Annie. She placed the black pen in Jack's hand. Jack then placed it on the flat metal surface of the press he had just gotten up from.

"Watch," Jack said, as he placed his hand about ten inches from the pen. He slowly contracted his fist, and when the fist was fully contracted the pen flew and stuck to the side of Jack's hand.

"Fascinating!" Abbie said.

"Wow, is that the extent of it? Can you generate a more powerful field than that?" Annie said.

"Yes," said Jack.

"Show me," Annie said.

Jack walked to the center of the lab and bent down on one knee. He pulled his arms in close, and then started to contract every muscle in his body as hard as he could. The effect didn't take long. Immediately the fluorescent lights, which were hanging down from the ceiling, started to lean towards Jack, as if being pulled towards him by an invisible string. Small things that were on the lab tables, such as instruments, beakers, scales started to fly through the air towards Jack. Drawers to the cabinets opened on the sides facing Jack. Glass was breaking. Metal banged off the floor and other objects and all of it, everything eventually, stuck to Jack.

"Okay! Okay! Okay! That's enough. Stop!" screamed Annie.

Jack relaxed his muscles and stood up. Everything that was stuck to him fell off onto the floor. He started to clean himself off by swiping his hands across his shirt and pants. He looked up at Annie and her sister.

"See what I mean?" Jack asked.

"That's unbelievable. I could make a life's work of testing and trying to understand what I just witnessed," Abbie said to Jack and her sister.

"Unfortunately, we don't have the time right now to study it further. We just have to document it, and let them know about it," Annie said to her sister.

"We need to get this guy a superhero name," Abbie said. "I would call him Superman, but that name is taken, and even Superman didn't generate his own gravity. That's some next level shit!"

"How about Density?" Annie asked.

Chapter 14

Jack woke with a start. They gave him a pillow and a blanket. Lotta good the pillow did, but at least it was something. He was laying on the ground next to a small bed. The bed was made of wood, and Jack saw no point in destroying it by lying on it. He didn't get up right away, though. Still sleepy, Jack closed his eyes tightly and rubbed them. It seemed like he had only been out a few minutes, but Jack looked down at his wristwatch and almost five hours had gone by. The long trip must have worn him out more than he realized.

The room was very dimly lit. A small blue light on top of an air purifier next to a table was the only light source. It cast the entire room in a pale blue light. As Jack slowly let his eyes survey the room he suddenly realized he wasn't alone. He could see the legs of a female in a knee-length skirt sitting in a chair next to the table. Suddenly, she spoke.

"Did you realize your body makes a type of low humming sound when you sleep? I couldn't figure out where it was coming from for the longest," she said.

"No, I didn't realize that," replied Jack, as he sat up and faced her. Jack recognized her voice as the woman that was in the meeting room he was in earlier ...the one who warned him that Karen wasn't safe no matter where Jack told her to go.

"I wanted to talk to you, Jack ...away from the others," she said in a calm but tired voice.

"Yeah?"

"Your grandfather Sebastian Coe is still alive. I know where you can find him."

"Who are you?" asked Jack.

"My name is Janet Houser. I am a US Senator from the state of Vermont." She sat up a little and reached to turn on a light on the desk next to her. Even though it was a small desk lamp, it completely illuminated the small room they occupied. *She's an attractive woman for someone who had to be in her sixties,* Jack thought. *Nice body. Cute haircut that showed off her still pretty face.*

"How do you know my grandfather is still alive?"

"Once I learned that you were real, I had people research it for me. He's living in Dallas, Texas. Retired. Goes by the name of James Watson now."

Janet Houser placed her hand on a note on the desk next to her and pushed it towards Jack.

"Here is his address. He might be able to give you some more answers."

Jack stood and stretched a little. Took the note off the table. Looked at it, and put it in his jacket pocket.

"I was hoping I would wake up and the last twenty four hours would have been a dream," said Jack, as he rubbed his eyes looking down at Janet.

"I'm afraid it's quite real. Surreal maybe, but quite real."

"I'm gonna get this guy ...this Mellig," said Jack.

"I hope so, Jack. For all of our sakes." Janet stood up and looked up into Jack's eyes. "Would you follow me? I would like to show you something."

Jack followed Janet out into the lobby in front of the elevator. When she got to the reception area she turned around and faced Jack.

"Jack, I wasn't kidding when I said he will use your family against you. He has my family, and this is the only way I can save them. You are the only one that can stop him. Find a way to stop him, please."

Janet opened up her jacket showing multiple sticks of explosives strapped to her waist with a mesh of wires coming out the top. Jack's eyes widened with shock. He noticed she had a switch in her hand with her thumb hovering just over a red button. His eyes shot back to her face.

"Okay, Okay... Hold on!" Jack said as he held out both of his hands with fingers spread wide.

"Don't do this Janet. There's another way. There's always another way."

Tears welled in Janet Hauser's eyes and then rolled down her cheeks.

"I'm sorry Jack..." Then, there was a blinding explosion. The force of the explosion blew Jack back against the wall next to the elevator. The wall came down on top of him, and he could feel other rubble piling up on top of the wall. He heard screaming from close by and screams from far away. Rocks, rubble and slabs of cement continued to fall and move for another twenty seconds or so. After that silence.

When the noise stopped Jack found himself lying prone under a giant slab of cement. He could feel the weight of it, but it didn't hurt him. He placed his hands next to his shoulders and did a push up to give him some room. Getting his feet under him, he stood up and pushed the giant slab of cement aside like it was made of cardboard. The exterior walls of the building were largely intact. However, when he looked up he could see the sky. He had been on a sub ground floor. The blast had not only blown up the floor he was on, but also the floor above, as well as the roof of the building. All he could see was smoking rubble, dust, bodies, and blood everywhere.

"What the hell?" Jack asked himself out loud. "Jesus. ...The twins!" Jack said, looking in the direction of the laboratory. He jumped from where he was in front of what was once the elevators to where the lab was. He didn't see a sign of them. Didn't hear anything. Jack started to move large slabs of brick and cement from the pile of debris that was once a laboratory.

"Annie? Abbie?" Jack said in a hopeful tone.

Finally, Jack moved one large slab of concrete that looked like it was a piece from the first floor of the building. It was wedged against the hydraulic press. There, laying under the press were Annie and Abbie. Dead.

"No! God dammit! No!" Jack said, vacillating between sheer anger and sadness. He bent down and put his hand on Abbie's leg. He liked these girls. He had made a connection with them, and more importantly they made him laugh for the first time in a long time. And now, they were gone. Jack was getting used to people he cared about suddenly being gone. He was tired of it. Each death strengthened his resolve to take Mellig down. Jack looked up towards the large bay door he entered the facility through. He could see a young man in a dark suit looking down at him. He had the tell-tale dull stare Jack was used to by now.

Jack yelled at the man. "Hey!"

The man in the dark suit turned and started to walk briskly down the alley towards the street. Remembering how he had previously jumped in front of the bus, Jack bent down and jumped, exploding upward like a rocket. He had tried to judge his trajectory so he would land in front of the man before he got to the street. As he was coming down into the alley, he realized he wasn't going to land where he wanted. Jack crashed into the first floor of the building on the opposite side of the building he had just jumped out of. Fortunately, he didn't miss by much. Jack found himself standing about three feet from the exterior wall. He stepped out into the alley through the ten feet wide hole he had just created.

"Hey! Why did you have to kill all those people, you piece of shit?" Jack said as he stood squarely in front of the man in the dark suit.

The man in the dark suit was youngish, maybe early twenties. About six feet tall with dark hair and pale skin. He began to smile.

"Why? Because they were plotting against me of course. They thought this place was a secret. But, I've been aware of it from the beginning. I knew they were looking for you. So, I let them look. Maybe they could find you. And, they did! And now they are dead. It's my lucky day that you got to see them die, Jack. That's what happens to those that oppose me" said the young man.

Jack took a step towards the man. "You are going to die."

"Easy, Jack. I found someone that wants to say hi to you. I'll be in touch..." And, with that, the young man looked down at the ground and took a few staggering steps back. "What? Where am I? Who are..."

Jack reached forward and grabbed the man by the shoulders to steady him. "What's your name?" asked Jack.

"Carl.'

"Well, Carl, you are standing in an alley in a shitty part of Chicago next to a building that just got blown up. Oh, and you have got an implant in your head that allows someone to take control over you whenever they want. Can you do me a favor and call 911. I've gotta go..."

Chapter 15

Jack sat on a short brick wall outside a McDonalds. Chomping on a Big Mac while watching a cricket next to his boot, he was lost in thought. He had finally found help. Other people. Powerful people that could speed his path to Mellig. To help him take the monster down, and now what? He was back to square one. He had a little more knowledge now, and knew more about his adversary. He even had the name and address of his grandfather. But, let's face it, he needed their help to find Mellig. Now he was back to flying blind. Jack was thinking about what the young man in the alley said. "I found someone that wants to say hi to you." Was he talking about Karen? The thought of it sent a bolt of anger through him. Then he had an idea.

Jack pulled out the burner phone he had purchased at the convenience store. He then produced the small piece of paper the kid gave him at the truckstop, the kid he saved from the bikers. The kid that wasn't that far away if he went to school at DePaul. He dialed the number.

"Hello," said the familiar voice of the young computer hacker.

"Hey, you probably didn't think you would ever hear from me again, but I need your help. Oh, I'm the guy that saved you from getting your ass kicked at the truckstop."

"Superman! Hell yes I remember you! Of course, I'll help. What do you need?"

"We can't do it over the phone. We need to meet."

An hour later, Jack sat on a metal bench next to Lake Michigan. He wore a black hoodie he had just purchased from a convenience store. The hood was pulled tight down over his head. He was eating a ham and cheese sandwich purchased from the same store. Jack figured it was at least two days old considering that the bread tasted like what he imagined cardboard to taste like. He was hoping beyond hope this young man, this computer nerd could help him find a way to take the next step.

Hearing footsteps, he turned his head to the left and saw the young man he had met at the truckstop striding towards him along the path that hugged the lake. When their eyes met the young man smiled.

"Superman?" said the young man as he stood next to Jack.

"Call me Jack please. Hello, Steve. It was Steve right?" asked Jack.

"That's right," said Steve, as he removed his backpack and took a seat next to Jack.

"It's a good thing I live in Chicago, otherwise this would have been a mega favor." .

"Oh, it's still gonna be a mega favor. But it benefits you too."

"Sorry about this, but I have to check something out on you." Jack removed the small credit card shaped device he got from the resistance group and placed it near the back of Steve's head. The light showed green.

"That's a goddamn miracle," said Jack.

Steve was examining the device as Jack removed it from the back of his head.

"What is that? Why did you put it on my head? What's going on?"

"It tells me if you had been contaminated ...if they had gotten to you."

"If who had gotten to me?"

"Um. Okay, let me just do a reset on the last couple of days for you and bring you up to speed," Jack said, and then went on to tell him everything. The reason for the blood tests. His family getting killed. The shot Karen gave him. His density and strength. The general. The chips in the back of the head. What the people look like when they are under control of the device. The giant explosion that killed his only help.

"Holy shit!" exclaimed Steve. "So, everyone I see every day some of them have this chip?"

"Yes they do. And, if they knew we knew each other you would have one too. ...so, heads up. This is the end of days stuff. It's risky and you could get hurt. Just letting you know up front. Are you ok with that?"

Steve thought about it for a minute. "Yep, I'm good with it."

"That's good, because if you said no, I was going to make you do it anyway," Jack said, half-joking.

"So, here's what I need. I need you to help me find the location of this general, or at least where he's controlling these people from. If we can at least limit his ability to control people that would be something. And, if we're lucky enough, we can get him at the same time."

Steve scratched his chin for a moment and stared out at the lake.

"Okay, well we should be able to do that," said Steve. "They are most likely using a radio wave on the electromagnetic spectrum. If that's the case, if you had two chips that were receiving broadcast signals simultaneously, then theoretically we should be able to triangulate the transmitters location."

"Two chips that are receiving the signal?"

"Yes, they have to be under control of the chip at the time," said Steve.

"Gotcha ...bunch of mind-controlled people. Same spot. Judging by what I experienced at a recent burger place that shouldn't be too hard."

"How long will it take you to get together what equipment you need?" asked Jack.

"Maybe a couple of hours. I have to swing by the electronics lab at the school," said Steve.

Chapter 16

"A Bears game? We are going to do this at a Bears game?" said Steve, as he sat next to Jack at the top row of Soldier Field. The stadium was packed. It was Packers week, so the stadium was 75% black and red, and 25% green and yellow.

"It's just what popped into my head. We are in Chicago, after all. But now that I'm here I'm not so sure it was my best idea," said Jack.

"Why?" Steve asked.

"Because there's a shit load of people ...and TV cameras."

"Jack, we can find another place," Steve said.

"No. Fuck it. We're here, and we don't have time to be dicking around. We'll do it here."

Steve had a black duffel bag sitting on his lap. He was obviously nervous, because his right knee was going up and down about fifty miles an hour.

"What are you going to do to get them to switch on the chips?" Steve asked.

"Something stupid," Jack replied. "How long will it take you to get your equipment ready and out?"

"Maybe forty-five seconds." Steve answered.

"Once it's out how long to triangulate a location?" asked Jack.

"Assuming there's at least two people with chips they are controlling, maybe forty-five seconds.

"When you have a location, take your ball cap off," said Jack.

Jack leaned over and whispered in Steve's ear, "Be discreet. Remember, the guy next to you could have an implant. Anyone around us. Once they are under their control, they are capable of anything. I don't want you getting thrown off the back row of the stadium."

"Wait, is that a realistic possibility?" Steve said while whipping his head around to look at the people sitting next to him.

"These people killed my entire family, and I told you about the place they just blew up, killing at least two hundred people. They will kill you too if they knew we were friends ...or put a chip in your head," said Jack emphatically.

"Just be careful. Act like it's no big deal and they won't think it's a big deal. Jack said. You ready?"

Steven nodded.

Jack looked down at the field. They were introducing the starting line up of the Bears. There was a semicircle of black and red balloons the players were running through. Beyond that were the cheerleaders. The team was waiting on about the 40 yard line for each player to run out to them. Jack stood up. It was kind of windy on the top step. He walked to the aisle, and down a few steps. He looked back at Steve and nodded.

"Ready or not..." Jack whispered to himself. With that, he bent down and jumped up like he was shot out of a cannon. Jack propelled through the air in a high elliptical arch. It occurred to Jack on his way down that he may actually land on top of someone. At his current approach to the field, he was headed for the mass of Bears players huddled in near the middle of the field. He quickly kicked his right let out twice to alter his approach.

Jack landed about ten yards away from the Bears players towards the opposing sideline. The impact was loud and massive. The field was moist, so the impact drilled Jack shin-deep beneath the surface of the field. He put his right hand down to steady himself, and pulled his feet out of the hole he made. His hoodie flew back off his head during the jump, so there he was. Jack Strong. Standing next to the

Chicago Bears football team in front of God, the stadium, and the TV cameras.

"What the hell man?" said a large Chicago Bears lineman as the entire team and the cheerleaders that were standing on the field were now staring at Jack. Policemen were now on a dead run from the sideline towards Jack.

"Where did you come from?" said a Bears player loudly.

Jack recognized him instantly. It was the starting quarterback.

"I came from the future. You'll be benched soon because you throw too many god damned pics." Suddenly, Jack noticed the quarterback's look had changed. He was still staring at Jack just as before, but now he had the familiar blank stare that Jack was used to seeing. As he glanced further around, the players and cheerleaders huddled around him fully three quarters of them had the same blank stare.

"Hello, Jack," said a voice behind Jack. Jack had heard that voice before. It was coming from a different person, but it was the same slow drawl. Jack turned. It was a policeman. He had his gun out of it's holster.

"How nice of you to drop in. What are you up to, Jack? This is a little aggressive for you isn't it? Now the whole world will know who you are."

"Just thought I would try to enjoy a little Sunday afternoon football. What's the gun for?" asked Jack.

The policeman looked down at his hand holding a gun. "Oh this? Death follows you until you join us. You should know that by now. I thought I might have this man kill himself today ...or, maybe kill her."

The policeman raised his arm and pointed the gun at one of the cheerleaders. Jack quickly reached his arm up, covering the end of the gun with his hand. The gun fired loudly into Jack's hand. There were screams from many of the cheerleaders. Jack took the gun away from the policeman, and then shoulder checked him, sending him flying back. Jack then bent the gun in half like it was made of clay.

"What the fuck is going on? Who the hell are you?" said one of the football players who clearly wasn't implanted with a chip yet. Jack looked up where Steve was sitting. He was taking his hat off and putting it back on his head in an exasperated fashion. Over and over. Bending down, Jack again jumped and shot up towards Steve, who was still sitting on the top row. He landed with a crack on the stairs about seven seats down from Steve. The cement under Jack's feet cracked, but it held. Jack stood up and looked at Steve, who pointed towards the scoreboard. His expression was that of pure disbelief in what he was seeing. Then Jack glanced at the scoreboard. In giant white letters on a black screen, it read DON'T GO JACK. Then he looked around and the entire stadium was looking at him, most had the blank stare of being controlled. They all began to chant, "Don't go, Jack. Don't go, Jack..."

There were police officers running up the stairs towards where Jack had landed.

Jack took a step towards Steve and grabbed a man standing next to Steve by the jacket, lifting him up so his face was right in front of him. He looked into the dull blank eyes of the man.

"Who wants to meet me?" Jack screamed.

The man's face broke into a broad creepy grin. "Karen, of course."

Jack gritted his teeth and tossed the man back towards his seat. He took two big steps, grabbed Steve's bag in one hand, put his arm around Steve with the other arm and lept over the back of the stands. Jack landed with a thud. Steve immediately dropped to his knees and vomited.

"Oh my god. Uggg. Oh my god," Steve blurted out between spitting on the ground.

"It's like I'm all of a sudden living in *The Twilight Zone*. Or, in that pod person movie. I wasn't sure if you were bullshitting me about these chips ...but it's true! Oh my god! It's all true!"

"Suck it up," said Jack as he helped Steve to his feet. "We need to get out of here and find these fuckers."

"No ...no. I, I can't. I gotta go home. I can't do this anymore," said Steve in a defeated tone between spitting on the ground.

"Sorry, bud, but they've seen you now. The safest place for you is with me," said Jack, as he picked up Steve's bag carrying the location device.

"Let's get out of here."

Chapter 17

Jack and Steve drove for approximately forty-two minutes on Jack's bike, going south from the stadium. They found a small walk-up burger joint along a farm to market road, looking like it had been there no less than fifty years. There was one pickup parked to the right of the building. The young woman at the register who served them had a white uniform with a white cap that said Jim's Burgers in red letters. She looked to be in her early twenties. Dark hair. Freckles. *Cute,* Jack thought, *in a rural country little sister sort of way.* There was another girl behind her standing over the fry machine, hands on her hips staring down into the grease. Looked like she was waiting for the cook cycle to complete. Jack wanted to know if either one of the girls had a chip, so he introduced himself loudly by name when she handed him her food.

"Nice to meet you, Jack! Hey let me ask you a question. If your best friend slept with your boyfriend, but your boyfriend is kind of a jerk, and you really liked your best friend and wanted to still be friends with her, what would you do?" the burger girl asked energetically.

"Ummm. I guess you could still be friends with her ...but now at least you know you can't trust her with boyfriends, right?" said Jack as he took the burger tray.

"That's true! My horoscope said I would get wisdom from a stranger today ...and you are that stranger Jack!"

Jack started to walk off with the food, but she stopped him.

"Hey, Jack. You want to know the crap of the story?"

Jack nodded. "Sure. What's the crap of the story?"

The girl at the register gave a half-turn, and pointed at the girl standing over the fry machine.

"That's the best friend I was referring to," the girl said, arching her eyebrows while looking at the girl over the fryer.

The fry girl looked up at Jack with a failed grin.

"Wow, didn't see that one coming," said Jack, looking at the fry girl. Then he raised his finger at the fry girl. "Watch out. You've got some payback coming..."

Steven had his location device set up on a picnic table next to the burger joint.

"Did they have chips?" asked Steve.

"No. They had a kinda juvenile *Young and the Restless* soap opera vibe, but no chips," Jack answered.

Jack stood next to him. He took out a burner phone from his jacket pocket and dialed a number.

"...Karen? ...Karen? Is that you?"

"Yes, it's me. Oh my god, Jack. Oh my god. I would have called you, but didn't know the number for your burner phone."

"Are you okay?"

"They came, Jack. They came and they took me from the lake house. They brought me to a place. Seemed like it was underground ...and, then just like that they just let me go," said Karen in a frightened voice.

"Where are you right now?"

"I'm sitting at a Starbucks in Wichita, Kansas. Thank god you called."

"Are your parents okay?" Jack asked.

"I don't know. They took me so fast."

"All right. Get a hotel room and text me the address. I'll be there soon."

"I love you Jack. Please hurry."

"Love you too."

Jack looked over at Steve, and Steve spoke up "You know they will be waiting for you if you go down there, right? You know she has a chip in her head, right?"

"Yeah, I know," said Jack, as if resigned to the thought.

"Hey I've been thinking about these chips. I think we can block the signal of anyone that might have one implanted. You see this?" Steve held up a little flat metallic looking thing about this size of a quarter.

"This little thing can block electromagnetic wave signals, but only for about a couple of feet. But, check this out. I fixed them to the back of a couple of ball caps ...so, you put the cap on their head and no more creepy zombie mode."

"That's fucking brilliant!" Jack exclaimed. "Remind me to give you a raise."

"But you don't pay me anything," Steve responded.

Jack sat on the seat of his bike, which was parked near the table Steve was sitting at. The bike creaked under Jack's weight.

"I'm sorry I called you, man. I just was running out of moves to make."

"What do you mean?" Steve asked.

"You are in this now. They've seen you with me. You can't go back ...not to school, not to your home. Not until this is resolved in some way."

"How exactly will it be resolved?"

"Gonna get my girl back first. Next, we find and destroy their ability to broadcast to these chips. Then, I kill the general ...then, it should be resolved."

"I'll be the one hiding behind the rock," Steve said.

"So, do you have the coordinates of the place?" Jack asked.

"Yeah!" said Steve studying his laptop. He then held it up for Jack to see the screen. "It appears to be within 100 yards or so of this building in Fort Worth, Texas," said Steve pointing to the screen.

"Fort Worth, huh?"

"Yep. So, we're going to Texas," said Steve, taking a bite of his burger.

"Kansas City is on the way to Texas." said Jack.

Chapter 18

Jack and Steve arrived in Kansas City around five thirty in the evening. It had just rained and the streets had a thin layer of water still draining. Jack had received a text from Karen around three thirty pm asking him to meet her at a Starbucks, she gave the address. Karen wasn't returning the texts Jack had sent after that. She gave no other reason for meeting her there, and Jack was uneasy about it. He knew it was a set up, but in spite of that he had to find a way to get Karen out of there without hurting her, or anyone else.

"What are we doing?" Steve asked as Jack pulled into a parking garage about a half a block down the street from the coffee shop.

"I want to get our plan straight before we just walk up there," Jack said, as he kicked the kickstand down and stood the bike up.

"We know it's a trap," Steve said.

"Yep, for sure. But, the main goal here is to get Karen out of here safely. They've seen you, but perhaps not as clearly as they know me. Pull that hood over your head and keep your head down," said Jack as he motioned towards Steve's hoodie.

Jack held his arm up showing Steve his phone with a picture of Karen. "This is what Karen looks like. I want you to go into the coffee shop. Buy a cup of coffee and sit behind Karen somewhere if possible. Got it?"

"Yep."

"You have the hat with the thingy on there?"

"Yep, right here." Steve pulled a hat out of his hoodie pocket.

"Good. When the time is right I want you to walk up and put it on her head."

"Okay. How will I know when the time is right?"

"There will be an announcement over the loudspeaker."

"What?"

"You will just know all right? Keep your wits about you. We don't know what this general has in store."

About fifteen minutes later, Jack was walking towards the coffee shop. Steve had left about eight minutes before him. The Starbucks was located on a fairly busy street. As Jack approached from across the street he could see Karen sitting alone at a table on the patio near the guard rail that separated the store from the street. He could see her face, and tell it wasn't her behind her eyes. Seeing this sent a momentary bolt of anger throughout Jack. Quickly, he stole a glance into the store and saw Steve sitting at a bar inside the shop front window facing out. Steve gave him a quick, small nod. Jack entered the patio through the open gate. He stopped about four feet in front of the table where Karen was sitting looked down, waiting for eye contact. Karen's vacant eyes slowly rose to face Jack, and the same creepy grin Jack had seen before spread wide across Karen's face.

"You are six minutes late and for that, your girl gets a knife in the hand." The voice came from Karen's mouth, but it wasn't Karen.

Karen's right hand quickly rose from under the table and stabbed her left hand, which was laying flat on the table. The lady sitting next to Karen let out a loud scream and jumped up from her table knocking the chair down as she ran inside the store. Others were gasping nearby.

"You mother fucker!" screamed Jack as he took a step towards Karen.

Karen quickly removed the knife from her hand and placed it next to her neck.

"Easy, Jack, or I'll kill this little bitch right here," said Karen.

"Don't you fucking dare," exclaimed Jack.

"You know, I think this is the longest I've ever actually sat in one of these bodies. It's strange really. I mean I can see through her eyes. I can speak through her ...but, there are things I can't do. Such as feel pain, obviously."

"You are insane," said Jack.

"Insane?" Karen belts out a loud laugh. "Possibly ...but you haven't asked me the real question. The most important question. Why. Why am I doing this? I'm going to tell you because I want you to understand."

"Okay, why then?"

"I must have ...I have to have control. It's about control. I absolutely can't stand not being in control. You see, Jack, I'm cursed. Cursed with the knowledge and vision of what's best for everyone. For humanity."

"Cursed, huh? Right... Control of what?" asked Jack as he watched blood drip from his girlfriend's hand into a growing pool below the table.

"Of what? Of everything! Do you realize when I do control everything there will be no more wars, no more famine. When I control everything everyone will be happy. The way it should be! Don't you see Jack?"

"You're a fucking idiot. There will be no more free will either." said Jack.

"Free will is overrated. And most don't know what to do with it anyway. It's this issue of control that has my focus directed at you, Jack. Do you realize you are the only one on this planet that I can't have direct control over? In a perfect world I would just chip you and I could use your magnificent skills at my pleasure ...so, I must find a way to control you indirectly. Otherwise, I must kill you."

"Actually someone did tell me that once. Right before you had them all killed ...and, you will never control me," Jack said, through clenched teeth. His anger was seething.

Karen laughed again. "I'm controlling you right now, Jack. You don't dare take another step towards your girlfriend out of fear I'll plunge this knife in her neck. Your girlfriend is mine, Jack. Mine forever more, and as long as I have her I control you."

Quite a crowd had gathered within twenty feet or so of Jack and his girlfriend. Jack could hear whispers of "It's the guy from the Bear's game" and "It's him" from the crowd. Many had their cell phones out, recording whatever was about to ensue. Just then a policeman came through the crowd and stood behind the iron fence facing Karen. He held his hands out, as one would when pleading for someone to remain calm.

"Just take it easy. Everyone take it easy. Please put the knife down, miss," the policeman said.

Jack noticed Steve had slowly made his way behind Karen, and was standing in the crowd of people backed up to the store. Steve then lunged forward and slapped the cap on Karen's head. The vacant stare on Karen's face vanished immediately. She dropped the knife on the table. Looked up at Jack with a look of utter terror. "Jack?" she said.

Then she looked down at her bloody hand and cradled it in her right hand. "Jack what is going on! Why is my hand bleeding! Oh my god it hurts!"

"That's a nice trick," said the policeman, who now had the same vacant stare on his face Karen just had on hers.

"You guys are smarter than I gave you credit for. But, we'll deal with that later," the policeman said as he reached into his holster, pulled out his pistol, and pointed it at Steve.

"Say goodbye to your friend Jack," said the policeman calmly. There were screams from the crowd.

Steve looked at Jack. "Jack, do something!" he yelled.

Jack raised both his hands, closed them into fists, and squeezed them harder than anything he could remember squeezing before. Immediately items nearby Jack began to fly through the air and cling to Jack's fists. The knife from the table Karen used to stab herself.

The policeman's gun. All manner of jewelry from nearby women. Forks and knives from tables. Even tables began to screech on the ground as they moved towards Jack. Once Jack saw the policeman no longer had his gun, Jack released the tension in his fists, and all the items that were attached fell to the ground.

"That's an even nicer trick!" said the policeman, as he looked at Jack with a crazy grin. He took a moment to process what he'd just seen. "Your density generates its own gravitational pull. Who would have thought... Okay.

"Enough talk. I've brought some friends of mine along with me. They were from a project I worked on after I created you Jack. They have been tested in battle many times, and have exceeded expectations on every occasion. I expect no less from them this time. I will give you one last opportunity, Jack. Join us. Join us, or die right here, right now on this street."

Jack heard metallic footsteps walking through the parking lot to the right of Starbucks. They grew louder and louder until Jack could finally see what was creating the footsteps. Two seven foot tall silver robots shaped like men were walking directly towards him. They were big and heavy looking. Their heads had no faces. Just a slit where the mouth should be for what Jack presumed was for audio. And it looked like some kind of LED lights where a face would have eyes. The crowd that had gathered parted for them, and they stopped about ten feet from Jack as if they were awaiting orders. Just then, two more of the androids jumped off the roof of Starbucks onto the street behind the crowd that had gathered near the policeman. There were gasps from the crowd and they quickly scattered, leaving Jack, the policeman, Karen and Steve as the only people that hadn't backed away.

"These beautiful creations are stronger than you Jack. I've instructed them to escort you into our facilities. If you refuse, I've instructed them to kill you. I hope you have the sense to comply," the policeman said.

Jack reached down at his feet and picked up the policeman's gun, and handed it to Steve.

"Take Karen into the store. Maybe there's a first aid kit in there," Jack said as he pointed towards Starbucks.

"Jack! Maybe you should just go with them!" exclaimed Karen, as she walked backwards into the store being escorted by Steve.

"I'll be all right." said Jack as he sized up these machines. Jack felt pretty confident. He knew things the general didn't know. Such as the fact that he could bench press eighty tons, and his skin was harder than a diamond, for starters. Jack quickly surveyed the crowd standing up against Starbucks, then he looked at the crowd in the street. There was around a fifteen feet between the androids, Jack, and the policeman. The crowd was big and getting bigger.

"All you people... All of you need to back way up. Way way up. I don't want anyone getting hurt. Except for these guys..." said Jack motioning towards the androids.

Then Jack looked directly at the police officer, and spoke to Mellig. "I'm about to fuck up your precious machines."

People began to retreat. One of the androids walked up to Jack and put it's right hand on Jack's left shoulder. A voice came from the machine.

"Come with us, Jack Strong."

Jack raised his right hand to his shoulder and grabbed the android's wrist.

"I won't be complying with your request."

With that, Jack side stepped, and struck the android's right arm just under the shoulder with his left hand. The arm snapped off and fell in Jack's right hand like a wet metallic noodle. Jack then swung the right arm of the android once over his head, and using that momentum he then struck the android in the head with it's own arm. The android's head took off like a Babe Ruth home run shot down the street. What was left of the android then fell in the street where it stood.

Jack then took a quick step towards the next closest android. Still holding the arm of the disabled robot, Jack swung it and hit the robot in the back of the heel. The machine's leg flew up, and sent the android reeling. It fell backwards onto the pavement. Jack quickly stepped closer to the android's head. He kept the momentum from the arm swinging, and dropped it directly down on top of the android's head ...which pushed it inches deep into the payment, and disabled the machine. The lights where it's eyes should be slowly faded to black.

The other two androids pulled pistols from a compartment in their hips, pointed them at Jack and began firing into Jack's chest. The barrage of bullets bounced off Jack as quickly as they were hitting him. People ducked for cover. Windows were breaking in store fronts and in parked cars from the spray of bullets. Jack saw the android's pistol he had just disabled was sitting on the ground next to his foot. He quickly picked it up, and put two rounds in the head of one of the androids. Nothing. Both machines were still firing at him. Jack threw the gun to the ground and started on a dead run at the nearest android. He played linebacker in football. He knew how to tackle. Jack left his feet about four feet in front of the android. His shoulder made contact with the metal machine about where the solar plexus would be on a normal human being. Normally in football, this would result in the person being tackled to leave their feet and fall back on the ground with Jack laying victorious on top of him. In this case, the impact of Jack hitting the machine resulted in a three inch casm into the chest of the android. Seeing the damage, Jack put one foot on the lower body of the android, and with both arms pulled the upper portion of the machine. There was a tearing metal sound, and quickly the two halves were separated. Jack tossed the upper body in the direction of the policeman, which skidded to a stop inches before hitting his feet. The policeman looked down at the ripped apart upper body of the machine with a strange grin on his face.

Meanwhile the lone remaining android was still firing it's weapon at Jack, having no impact of course. Jack walked calmly towards the machine. Bullets bounced off of him like windblown sand at the beach. Reaching the machine, Jack placed his foot behind the androids leg, and then hit it in the chest. The machine tripped, falling hard to the ground. Jack then reached down, and with little effort, pulled the head from the machine. Then he took two steps and punted it like a football. The metallic head disappeared into the sky.

There was a moment of silence after the machines fell to the ground, and then there was a cheer from the crowd. Someone yelled, "That's amazing! What do we call you?"

Jack didn't say anything.

"You can call him 'Density,' said the dull-eyed policeman.

The policeman walked up to Jack. "I have to admit Jack, part of me was hoping you would best my androids. After all, you are my creation too."

"I'm coming for you," said Jack. "And give this poor man back his body."

Steve and Karen approached Jack from Starbucks. Karen had her hand wrapped in a white bandage. Jack and Karen embraced, and then kissed.

"Thank god you are all right," Jack said, as he gave Karen a tight embrace.

"This whole thing is freaking me the hell out!" Steve exclaimed as he whispered loudly in Jack's ear. "Anyone could have that chip! We aren't safe! Karen and I aren't safe!"

"I know," said Jack.

A woman from the crowd blurted out, "That's amazing! How did you beat them? Why didn't those bullets hurt you? What are you?"

"I'm just a science project."

Jack looked at Steve and Karen and spoke softly to them. "We have got to get out of here. I've got an idea. Follow me."

Jack grabbed Karen's hand and started walking towards the Starbucks parking lot.

"Those were four big heavy robots. They had to get them here somehow," Jack said as they walked briskly.

As they walked into the parking lot they could see a large military cargo transport parked in the alley. It was dark blue with blacked out windows.

"Bingo!" Jack said. "We should be able to use that to travel."

Jack walked up. Knocked on the drivers side glass. He motioned with his finger for the driver to step out.

"Step away from the vehicle," said the driver as he stepped out of the vehicle and drew his weapon at Jack.

"Dude, just give me the keys," said Jack, as he held out his hand.

The driver of the truck fired his weapon into Jack's chest.

"Really? So you would have just killed me for asking you for keys?"

Jack took two steps towards the driver and grabbed the gun out of his hand. He then held his hand out again, palm up. The driver appeared to know who Jack was, because he wasn't entirely in shock that the bullet bounced off Jack.

"Keys please," said Jack.

The drivers slowly reached into his pocket and dropped the keys into Jack's hand.

"You know, you should really think about changing jobs. You are willingly helping this asshole ...and that's bad. Or better yet, join the resistance," said Jack as he opened the back door to the van.

"Resistance?" inquired the driver. "You mean like *Star Wars*?"

"Exactly!" stated Jack emphatically. The driver appeared confused.

"So, are you guys the resistance?" asked the driver.

"Yes." Karen said.

"So, can I come with you?" asked the driver.

In unison Karen, Jack, and Steve all muttered an emphatic "No."

"Wait," Steve said.

"There's most likely a gps tracker on this vehicle. Let me locate it and disable it," said Steve as he pulled a piece of equipment out of his backpack.

Chapter 19

They had been driving for hours. Steve was at the wheel, whistling.

The inside of the cargo carrier had two thick metal benches along each side of the vehicle. Jack was sitting down along the drivers side of the vehicle. Karen was laying down with her head in Jack's lap, looking up at him. Jack had his head resting against the wall of the vehicle. For the first time in what seemed like days, he felt like he could take a breath. Relax a little bit. After all, he had his girl back. And, she was okay. Jack brought Karen up to speed on how he met Steve. Meeting the resistance people. The building getting blown up. The Bears game. And, their plan, such as it was to try and stop the general. But for the past twenty-five minutes he had been fast asleep.

"I didn't know you could do that gravity thing with your fists," said Karen.

Jack's head snapped with a start.

"I'm sorry, were you asleep?" Karen asked apologetically.

"I said I didn't know you could do that gravity thing with your fists."

"No, it's okay. Yeah...I didn't really know if it would work. I just did it, hoping it would work. He was going to kill Steve," said Jack as he stretched his legs out and yawned.

"I'm curious, what was it like? When he controlled your body. What was it like? Were you aware of it?" asked Jack.

"No. It's kind of like when you have surgery. Before the surgery you're talking to the doctor. Then boom, you wake up an hour later with no recognition that the hour had gone by. It's just like a blank space where time went by. Scary as hell basically," said Karen.

"How's your hand feeling?"

Karen looked at her bandaged hand and gently felt it with her right hand. "It hurts, but I think it will be okay. It will make a good story one day," she said with a smile.

"Are your mom and dad okay?" Jack asked hesitantly.

"I don't know. They came. They took me, and I don't know what happened to them. I've been trying to get in touch with them. The neighbor said there was no one home."

"I'm sure they are all right," said Jack, putting on a strong face, but knew there was some doubt as to whether they were alive. He turned his head towards the front of the vehicle.

"Hey, Steve, I'm starving. Can you find a place to pull over and eat?" asked Jack.

A few minutes later they were standing at the counter of a Dairy Queen in a small town in Oklahoma. Steve had parked the cargo transport in the rear and they had walked up. The Dairy Queen had eight to ten people in it, not counting the staff. Jack was always a big fan of Dairy Queen. He was a frequent visitor of the one in La Marque. There was a young man behind the counter. Couldn't have been more than sixteen years old. Acne scars on his face. Red Dairy Queen hat on his dark hair, tilted slightly off-center.

"Hello there. What can I get for you guys," the young man said as he scanned the faces of Karen, Steve, and Jack. Except his eyes stopped when he got to Jack, and his eyes widened.

"Hey! It's you! Density. You're Density. Right?" said the young man excitedly.

Jack looked at Steve and Karen in a slightly perplexed way.

"Dude! You are so so famous. Everyone is talking about you. You're everywhere!"

Five minutes later, the trio were outside munching on hamburgers. Steve and Karen sat at a table on a side patio, and Jack sat next to them on a curb. Steve was studying his cell phone.

"That kid was right. You are everywhere. Check it out. Here's the girl that sold us that food outside of Chicago."

Steve held up his cell phone video to Jack and Karen. It was news footage of a blond female reporter interviewing the girl from Jim's Burgers that Jack and Steve had visited.

"Bob, I'm standing here with Sandra Jacobs at Jim's Burgers in Winona. Sandra, what can you tell us about the man they call Density? You say you served him?" the female reporter asked.

"Oh yeah! He was here," said the girl wearing a white cap that said Jim's Burgers.

"Well, my horoscope said I would get wisdom that day, and what do you know, he gave me advice about my cheating boyfriend, and girlfriend. They cheated with each other, and he told me what to do ...and, did I mention he was triple hot!?"

The female reporter smiled and turned to the camera.

"Well there you have it. A superhero that is hot, and gives relationship advice."

Steve pulled his phone back. Karen let out a big laugh.

"When did you guys see that girl?" Karen asked.

"That was after the Bears game." Steve said.

"So what do we do now? Seems like we are traveling with one of the most widely recognizable people in the world. How are we going to slip into Fort Worth and blow shit up without being noticed." Karen asked.

"It doesn't change anything. We keep to the plan ...except I do want to make one pit stop before we go to Fort Worth," said Jack.

"What pit stop?" Steve said.

"I want to stop and see my Grandpa," said Jack, as he stuffed the last bit of his burger into his mouth and stood up.

Chapter 20

It was about seven thirty in the evening. The trio of Jack, Karen, and Steve were in a Dallas suburb less than a mile away from the address the woman gave Jack right before she blew herself and everyone else up in Chicago. Jack was appreciative the small piece of paper survived. *Minor miracle*, he thought. Steve had pulled the van into a Wal-mart parking lot down the street from the neighborhood where Jack's grandfather lived. He walked back towards the rear of the cargo van where Jack and Karen were sitting. He grunted and took a seat opposite them.

"You know there's a pretty decent chance that your grandfather is either implanted, or his house is under surveillance waiting for you to show up," said Steve.

"Yeah, I know. I was thinking about that too," said Jack.

"But, I gotta try to see him. He's my grandfather. But you and Karen should stay here. They can't hurt me, but they could hurt you. I'll just walk over there."

"Okay, have you thought about what you are going to say to him?" Karen asked.

"Not exactly. Just wanted to know about my birth mother and dad. Whatever he knows. And, also about General Mellig. He knew him. Maybe I can get some bit of info we can use to our advantage," Jack said.

"You can't leave until I run and get you a couple of things," Karen said, as she stood up, walked to the back of the van, unlocked the door and jumped out. Within ten minutes she was back with a plastic Walmart shopping bag in tow. Plopping the bag down in front of Jack, she reached in and pulled out a white hoodie and a hat.

"We need to keep your face hidden as much as possible. They have eyes everywhere, and anyone that's implanted could see you and locate us. Don't worry, I paid cash so they can't track my card," said Karen, as she leaned forward and gave Jack a quick kiss on the cheek.

"Thanks Kare," said Jack, as he slipped the hoodie on over his shirt and tucked the blue hat that had the white star of the Dallas Cowboys down low on his head. Then he pulled the hoodie over the hat. And so Jack walked out of the Walmart parking lot, and took a line that put him on the closest street adjacent to the Wal-mart. His burner phone's map said he would walk for three blocks straight, make a left turn, go two blocks and make a right. It was an older neighborhood. Large, mature trees in most of the yards. The homes were well maintained, and most people would call it a wealthy neighborhood. Lots of german-made cars.

Jack's hands were in his hoodie pockets. He found himself having to hold his arms forward a little, otherwise, if he let them hang naturally the weight of his arms would stretch the hoodie beyond its normal limits. *Being ten thousand pounds is a pain in the ass,* Jack thought to himself as he walked. Lost in his thoughts, Jack had one of those moments that time went by without him really realizing it. Suddenly, he was standing in front of his grandfather's house ...or, at least the address the senator gave him for his grandfather's house. Jack knocked on the thick, dark wooden door and took a couple of steps back. A few seconds later, it opened.

A short hispanc lady in a maid outfit answered the door.

"Jess?" she said, in a thick accent.

"Hello, I'm looking for James Watson."

"Meester Watson is resting now. Not seeing veesitors now. Sorry," she started to close the door.

Jack took a step forward and placed his hand on the door to keep it from shutting.

The maid looked Jack in the eyes with equal parts fear and anger.

"I think he'll want to see me. You see, I'm his grandson," said Jack.

"You go! I no care, you go!" said the maid angrily.

"I don't want to scare you, and I hate to be rude, but, I'm coming inside this house," said Jack, as he stepped forward again and opened the door.

The maid let out a scream, and ran down an adjacent hallway shouting "Meester Watson! Meester Watson! Meester Watson!"

Jack could hear a man raise his voice down the hall the maid just ran down. "Blazes woman, will you stop screaming? Just relax! I'm gonna see what's going on!"

A few seconds later, a white-haired man that looked to be in his mid to late sixties stepped briskly into the foyer. He was wearing a casual golf shirt and khaki trousers.

"What's the meaning of this! Who are you, and how dare you force your way into my house. What do you want!"

"I'm very sorry, sir," said Jack.

"Wait, I recognize you. I've seen your face before... on the news. Who are you?"

"My name is Jack. I think I may be your grandson."

"How... How did you find me, who sent you here.?"

"It was a US Senator from Vermont. She's dead now, but she gave me your address before she died, and told me you were my grandfather."

"Who are you with?" asked Mr. Watson as he poked his head outside the front door to check if anyone was there. He then shut the door quickly. "You shouldn't have come here," said Jack's grandfather as he stepped forward and put both his hands on Jack's shoulders.

"They told me you left me with a family in Texas. My name is Jack Strong."

"You really are him aren't you." said Jack's grandfather. He took a couple of steps back and his eyes wandered a bit. You could see he was going through the ramifications of Jack walking through his door.

"If you found me, it's just a matter of time before he does," said Jack's grandfather. "I'm so sorry, Jack. I'm so so sorry the way things happened with you, but under the circumstances it was the only thing I knew to do. It's my great loss that I couldn't be part of your life, but all in all your life was better than the alternative that was facing you at the time."

"I'm not here to make you feel bad. Or, give you some kind of guilt trip. I just wanted to meet my Grandpa. And, maybe learn some things from you ...like about my mom, and real dad."

Jack's grandfather called, "Maria, bring us some tea on the porch please."

"What meester Watson?" the maid said from the kitchen.

"Tea! Porch!" Fired James Watson.

Jack wasn't used to drinking tea in a cup, but a few minutes later, he was. James Watson sat under a covered porch overlooking a pool. Jack noticed there were some cinder blocks stacked by the fence and took it upon himself to stack three of them next to the table so he could sit next to his grandfather.

"Your father was a scientist, brilliant man. You got your height from him. Mellig found him early in his career, and funded his research on the Density Project. Of course, early on it wasn't called the Density Project. It was just cellular research Mark was doing. That was his name Mark Maddox; your dad's name. Once Mellig saw that Mark was on to something, he created the Density Project with Mark as the brains behind it."

"How did you know them? I mean back then, how did you know them?" Jack asked.

"At that time I worked in the Pentagon. I was a liaison between the General who was in charge of administering and allocating funds to top secret projects, and the congressional committee in charge of funding these type of research projects. So, I was familiar with the project, and Mellig, and Mark Maddox."

"How did my mom come into the picture?" asked Jack, as he finished off his tea and sat the cup gingerly back down on the saucer.

"Well, your mom, Susan ...that was her name, Susan. She had recently graduated from Brown University with a masters, and her field of study was cellular biology. And, I got her a job under Mark Maddox working on the Density Project. I didn't know that they would end up being a couple. But alas, that is where you came into the picture."

"So what happened? I mean, to kill my dad?"

"The project was successful on amphibians and small animals, and they were getting close to testing it on humans, but, there was some kind of accident in the lab. You see, the formula in it's undiluted form was very caustic, and quite lethal to breathe. Your father died instantly. Your mother, who was six months pregnant at the time was exposed as well, but less so. She didn't die instantly. They kept her alive in a hospital bed."

A tear welled in Jack's grandfather's eye. He reached to wipe it.

"Once Mellig found out you tested positive for the Density gene in vitro, there was no measure he was not willing to go to to keep your mother alive until she could give birth to you. Finally, at eight and a half months they took you. Your mother died shortly thereafter I am told. You see, the whole thing was top secret. They wouldn't let me see her."

"So, both my parents were scientists, and I ended up cutting and shaping metal for a living. How did I end up in Texas.?"

"When you were three months old, I found out through great effort where they were keeping you. I had a colleague of mine help me arrange a team to take you. Kidnap you as it were. Once we took you I arranged to place you with the father you grew up with. He was an old colleague of mine from my agency days. I just asked the biggest favor of him that I could, and he did it. He didn't even know your story. Just that your life would have been terrible, and he could give you a normal life ...and that no one could ever know how he got you"

Jack, looked away from his grandfather, and down into the blue water of the pool. "I see. I had a good upbringing. You did the right thing. I'm grateful to you for what you did for me."

Tears rolled down James' face as he stared at Jack, and nodded.

"Mellig is a maniacal egomaniac. When he lost you, he took a turn. His obsession to create all forms of weapons became all he cared about. And, once he got ahold of the chip he puts in peoples heads, that was it. He saw a way to put himself in charge of everything. And that's what he's been doing for the last five years.

You know they had that cell phone footage of you at the Bears gave all over the news. That was something."

"It was stupid is what it was. I was stupid for doing it."

"Why did you do that?"

"My friend and I found a way to triangulate the location of where the general broadcasts his signal to the chips, and it required multiple people under the chips control at one time in near proximity to us, ...so that's what came to my mind. Not the best idea I've had, but we did get the location."

"Really? Where is it?"

"It's in Fort Worth. I wanted to come see you on the way over there."

"What will you do when you get there?"

"I don't know. Destroy it. If Mellig is there, I will kill him. Speaking of that, you don't happen to have a picture of what he looks like do you?"

"I may. Let me check. Follow me," James said as he got up and went into the house.

Jack followed him into his study, where James opened a file cabinet and took out a folder. He flipped through some of its contents, and took out a five by seven colored photograph.

"Here, here is a picture of the project team. This was early when they first started." James pointed to the picture. "There's your mom, and there's your dad, and there is Mellig."

Jack was unprepared for the flush of emotion that overcame him briefly. Seeing a picture of this mom and dad caught him off guard. His mom was beautiful, he thought. Then his eyes rested on Mellig. Mellig had piercing eyes, dark hair, and that same crazy grin that he had seen on a couple of chipped people's faces from time to time.

"You keep that. Of all people, you should have that," said Jack's grandfather.

"I have another question. I'm guessing Mellig never knew it was you that took me when I was a baby. Otherwise, he probably would have killed you then. So, why did you end up changing your name?"

James took a deep breath and sat down on the edge of the desk in his study.

"When they implemented this blood test for young men I knew Mellig was behind it. I knew he was still looking for you. In the interest of self preservation I thought it was prudent to put another layer of obfuscation between me and him. So, I changed my name and moved from Virginia to Dallas.

And, I'll tell you something else. The hardest thing I've ever had to do in my life is resist the urge to look you up, to find out about you in Texas. I knew that would be very dangerous for you, and not in your best interest at the time."

Just then, both of them heard a loud gun shot, and a picture behind Jack's grandfather on the shelf exploded. Glass fragments and wood splinters suddenly were flying around the room. Both Jack and his grandfather looked at the door. Jack instinctively stood up in front of his grandfather, between him and the door to the study.

"Maria?" James Watson asked in a non believing tone.

The maid stood in the doorway to the study with her arm stretched out. Her thick, short, meaty fingers death gripped a small black Glock 43 pistol, pointed straight at Jack's chest.

"Git out da way you! I'm gonna kill him!" shouted the maid.

"Look at her!" Jack's grandfather said. "She must have had one of those chips in her head this whole time."

"No. She doesn't." said Jack.

"How? How do you know that?"

"Because I've seen enough people who have a chip to know what it looks like, and she doesn't have one. Or at least she's not being controlled by it now," Jack said as he took a few steps forward and took the gun away from the maid.

The maid dropped to her knees and began to cry into her hands.

James quickly made his way around Jack and bent down to Maria's level.

"This woman has worked for me for two years. Maria, why were you trying to kill me?" James Watson asked.

"They have my boy and Hector, my husband. They control dem. They said they would kill dem if I didn't kill you if your grandson ever showed up. And, he showed up." Maria said through her sobbing.

"I've seen this before," said Jack. "The general manipulates some people by threatening their loved ones. Sometimes he prefers not to chip people if it fits the situation. This means he knew you were here the whole time. He took advantage of her being here to watch you. To wait. To see if I would ever show up. You were just bait."

James stood up and looked out his study windows. He raised his arm and pointed. "Look," he said.

Jack, James, and even Maria, who by this time had stood up, were all looking out the window. All three moved closer to the window to see outside. There were between fifty and sixty people. Had to be people from neighboring houses. They were all standing outside James' house. Some were in the yard. Some were standing in the street. They all faced James' house. All of them had the blank wide eyed stare Jack had seen so many times. None of them moved. They stood still. Like motionless creepy living statues.

"That's what people with the chip look like," said Jack.

"Jesus, tell me that's not creepy," Jack's grandfather said.

"He's everywhere. We've got... I've got to stop this," Jack said.

As all three of them stood and looked at the hoard of entranced people in Jack's grandfather's front yard, James spoke up...

"Maria, you are fired. Get your stuff and leave."

"but, meester..."

James pointed at the door. "Get your stuff and leave!"

"But"

"Out!"

"Meester..."

James turned towards Maria. "Maria! Are you serious? You just tried to kill me. You are fired, get your stuff, and get out!"

Maria stomped off, and a moment later, exited the front door with her small black purse. She stepped onto the doorstep with great trepidation, monitoring closely any change in the entranced crowd.

In one voice, every person in James Watson's front yard and the street in front of his house spoke...

"Maria Cordova, you have failed," They all point towards the window at the same time, where Jack and his grandfather still stood. "James Watson lives. You have failed."

Maria again fell to her knees and began sobbing loudly into her hands. "I try. I try. ...I miss, I miss," she shouted through her sobbing

"We've got to get you out of here," said Jack to his grandfather.

"We can leave in my car. The garage is around the side," James Watson said.

"No. I weigh ten thousand pounds. I can't get in your car and, I'm not letting you go without me."

"Ten thousand? How then?" Jack's grandfather asked.

"I've got an idea."

Jack and his grandfather stood on the patio next to the pool. "I'm going to pick you up. Hold tightly to my neck. Keep your head down, and keep your tongue on the roof of your mouth."

"You're not telling me you can fly?" Jack's grandfather said emphatically.

Jack laughed. "No, I can't fly. But, it turns out I can jump really far. So, we are going to jump out of here. Okay?"

"Gonna jump? Can I say no?"

"We are jumping," Jack said.

"Okay. We are jumping. Gonna jump. Let's jump. Okay, Okay. Let's do it."

Jack picked up his grandfather, bent down, and shot into the air like he was fired from a rail gun in the direction of Wal-mart. Towards the apex of the jump Jack noticed his grandfather raised his head a little to steal a look, and then quickly put it back down. Jack just made the edge of the Wal-mart parking lot, landing in a manicured flower bed. There was a large black woman with a red dress, and a matching red hat putting groceries into her car nearby. Hearing the landing, she quickly spun around startled.

"What? Where did ya'll come from?" she said as Jack was standing his grandfather up, making sure he was alright.

"We came from the sky. It's raining men," said Jack, as he and his grandfather started to walk towards the parked transport.

Jack's grandfather started to whistle the tune "It's Raining Men." She looked to the sky, and then back at Jack. Then, she just turned around and continued to put groceries in her car while shaking her head.

She muttered to herself, "I know I didn't just see two grown ass white men fall from the sky."

Jack opened the back door to the blue cargo transport. Steve was lying prone on one side bench, and Karen was laying down on the other one. Steve sat up, startled, and let out a loud, "What?"

James Watson and Jack climbed up and entered the van. Jack closed the doors behind them.

"You guys, meet my grandfather. I'm just gonna call you grandpa to make it easy." Jack said to his grandpa. His grandpa nodded.

"This is Karen, and this is Steve."

Jack's grandpa nodded at each of them. "My pleasure." he said.

"What happened?" Karen said as she stood up and hugged Jack.

"Well, it was going great ...right up until the time the maid tried to kill Grandpa, and then about fifty of his neighbors turned into chipped-out zombies."

"What?!" Karen said.

"Yeah, they were just standing in his yard. Steve, it was like that movie you were talking about. I couldn't leave him there, so for now he's coming with us."

Chapter 21

Forty-five minutes later Jack and Karen were walking along a paved trail through a wooded park. The park was largely deserted on a workday in the afternoon. They had all thought it was a good idea to temporarily stay at the park while they formulated their next step.

Steven and Jack's grandpa had walked across the street to pick up some food at a Whataburger. The van was parked in the parking lot at the park. There was only one other car parked there.

"How's your hand?" said Jack, as he gently picked up Karen's hand to more closely inspect it.

It had a bandage wrapped around under her thumb and across her hand.

"I guess you would say I was lucky. The knife apparently missed any large blood vessels, and also missed the tendons because I can open and close my fingers." she said, as she opened and closed her fingers.

"We should have gone to a doctor."

"No! Too risky. Besides I've been through worse. Remember when I got my two front teeth knocked out trying to do a trick on my bike in second -grade?" said Karen.

Jack laughed. "Yeah. Look Ma, no teeth."

"Hey!" Karen punched him in the shoulder, and then immediately regretted it as she bent to her knees, holding her punch hand.

"I'm sorry." said Jack, as he bit his lower lip, knowing Karen was in pain.

"No, it's my fault. I forget you are cement man now. So, how's that gonna work when we.... you know."

"It's been a while hasn't it? You want to find out?"

"What now?" Karen asked, surprised. She was studying Jack's face to see if he was serious.

"I'm not sure its the best time or place," Jack said smiling. "But, let's try to pencil it in soon, okay." Jack gently put his hands on Karen's shoulders, and reached in and kissed her.

"I'm starving. Let's go back and see if they're back with the food," Jack said, as he grabbed Karen's good hand and began to walk back towards the parking lot."

Two hours later, Jack, Karen, Steve, and his grandfather stood atop a six story parking garage. Binoculars in hand, looking down at the building, Steve had identified the source of the chip signal. The cargo van was parked towards the far side of the parking garage, so as not to be seen from the street below.

"I really wish you guys had stayed back like I suggested," said Jack. "It's not safe here."

"There's no way I'm letting you do this by yourself," said Karen, putting her hand on Jack's shoulder as they looked at the building below them.

Jack looked over at Steve.

"What she said," said Steve, both hands resting on the chest-high barrier at the edge of the top level of the parking garage.

"So that building is the control center? For all these people with the chip?" asked Jack's grandfather.

"Yes. At least, that is the source of the control signal," said Steve, with a note of excitement.

"Either way, we need to put it out of business," Jack said, matter of factly.

From the group's vantage point, they could see two doors to the building, one on the narrow side of the building, and one larger one on the long side, although it wasn't centered. The entryway was down towards the end closest to the street. The building was large. Very large. An entire city block long, and about a half a block wide.

Looked to be two stories, although no telling what was below the building. The odd thing about the building is there were no windows. All brick facade, kind of a soft white peachy color to the bricks. Two uniformed guards stood next to the larger entry on the wide side of the building. They were both armed, although their pistols were holstered. Jack couldn't really tell, but from where he was standing it appeared the guards had the zombie chip stare.

Jack was nervous. Nervous because he felt like this was the culmination of something. Not only ending the ability for the general to control the chips, but also revenge for his mom and little brother. He wanted that more than anything. He had to do right by them, he thought. He had to exact justice. Generally, Jack wasn't a vengeful guy, but this was different. This was a whole other level. The kind of level that makes you have nothing else to lose. In his mind, it was just the right thing to do.

He didn't know what exactly he was looking for, but he knew one thing ...he couldn't just destroy the whole building. That would hurt or kill a lot of people. People that may not be there of their own volition. It's not like there was a lot of traffic into and out of the building. Since he had been watching, there had been a total of four people go into the building. No one had come out yet. ...except, wait a minute. The group watched as a man exited the building. The hair on the back of Jack's neck stood up because the guy was wearing a slim black suit with a skinny black tie over a white shirt. The exact same suit the assassin was wearing that killed his mom and little brother.

"You see that guy?" Steve asked.

"Yeah." answered Jack. "And, I'm gonna say hi to him."

The man in the back suit was headed towards a car parked nearby the building. It was now or never, Jack thought to himself. He sat the binoculars down on the ledge he was standing next to. Without thinking, he bent down and launched himself into the air.

By now he had learned to judge a little better how hard to jump based on how far he wanted to go.

"It's so weird when he does that," said Karen. "Kinda cool, though."

"I know. I wish I could do it," Steve answered.

With a giant meteor-like thud, Jack impacted the ground about fifteen feet in front of the man in the black suit. Chunks of asphalt from the parking lot created a roughly fifty-foot debris field. The tiny rocks could be heard several seconds later still pelting the building and other vehicles. Oddly the man in the black suit didn't panic that much, he just stopped in his tracks. Once he recognized Jack, he pulled a gun from his coat holster and began putting rounds on Jack. As if that would hurt him.

Jack quickly approached the man in the suit. Once he realized that he couldn't hurt Jack, the man in the suit turned around to run, but it was too late. Jack already had him by the jacket, and proceeded to pull him in and bear hug him. Then, bending down, Jack again shot himself into the air towards the parking garage.

The landing on the parking garage wasn't as violent as the parking lot because the landing point was near the apex of the jump. He hadn't built up speed on the way down yet. Jack threw the guy down on the ground.

The man in the suit pushed himself up, staggering a little bit.

Jack pointed at the cargo van.

"Back of the van. Now!"

The man in the suit complied, and briskly walked towards the back of the blue cargo van. Karen, Steve, and Jack's grandfather followed behind Jack towards the back of the van.

"What..." Karen started to say, but noticed Jack quickly turned and put his finger to his lips. Jack didn't want the man in the suit to hear any conversations between them that may change any answers he would give.

Jack walked up to the guy in the suit and started to pat him down. He pulled a Glock 17 from his belt and a Glock 43 from an ankle holster. Handed them to his grandfather. Then Jack took a step back and looked the guy in the eyes.

"I need to know two things about that building. How many people are in there, and where exactly is the control center where they control the chips?"

"I'm not disclosing any of that to you. I'm not telling you anything," said the man, with a slightly fearful tone as he took a step away from Jack. "And, what do you mean chips?"

That last part pissed Jack off even more. Jack smiled and extended his hand.

"Let's take a step back. I haven't introduced myself properly. My name is Jack Strong."

The man in the suit instinctively raised his hand to shake Jack's hand. Jack grabbed it quickly. The man in the suit tried to pull away, but there was no getting away from Jack's grip.

"You see, the thing is I don't have a lot of time, Black Suit Guy, and I have even less patience right now."

Jack looked down the guy's hand. "Is this your trigger pulling finger?"

With his left hand Jack, grabbed the guys index finger and gave it a good tug. The finger came off like it was made of silly putty.

The man in the suit screamed in agony.

"Oh my god!" Steve belted out in shock.

"I'll ask again. How many people are in the building, and where do they control the chips from?"

"You pulled my finger off, mother fucker!"

"Yes I did," Jack said as he grabbed the guy's thumb with his left hand. "Most people say they would prefer the thumb to a finger. Let's find out if it hurts just as much as the finger."

"No! Wait! Good god. All right. There's probably three hundred people in there. Mostly operators and monitors, and I hate to break it to you but the entire first and second floors of that building are set to monitor and operate the chips."

Jack let go of the guys hand and walked back over the edge of the parking garage to take another look at the building below. He didn't give a care about the guy behind him. After all the guy couldn't hurt him. The main concern for Jack was he didn't want to kill anyone he didn't have to ..but, one way or another he was going to destroy their ability to control those chips. And, then it occurred to him...

Jack quickly bent down and jumped again. The air made a whistling noise in his ears as he coursed through the arch of the jump. He landed with a giant thud about thirty feet in front of the side door. The asphalt sprayed nearby cars.

The two droned out guards at the gate immediately got their pistols out and began firing at Jack. Calmly walking towards the front door and up the steps, Jack didn't want to hurt the guards because he could tell they were under someone else's control. The bullets bounced off him like tiny pebbles against a semi truck.

"You guys get a pass today. I can tell you just arn't feeling yourselves. Just stay out here. I don't want to have to hurt you," said Jack, as he opened the door.

It had occurred to Jack a moment before that he didn't have to hurt anyone. He thought, *Why do I need to be in a hurry and hurt people if they can't hurt me.* He had made up his mind to methodically destroy every machine in that building. And, on the off chance he came face to face with the general, then he would definitely have to take him out.

Inside the double doors, the entire floor was a shiny white marble.There was a modern art statue standing about eight feet tall just in front of him. Some kind of grey welded metal thing. Jack wasn't a fan. *Looks stupid, waste of money,* Jack thought to himself. To his left was a single brown door. Other than that there was one long single story wall that ran the entire width of the building.

To Jack's right there was a reception area with a lone woman manning the counter. She was a large woman wearing a white dress, with an off white shawl pulled over her shoulders. Must have been in her mid-forties, Jack thought. Dark hair worn down past her shoulders, straight. Black glasses on. Her eyes widened a bit as Jack approached her.

"All this, and here you are sitting here without an active chip. That surprises me," said Jack.

"Chip? I'm just a temp. I..., I don't know what you mean. Am I supposed to have a chip? They didn't tell me about a chip. Were those guys shooting at you?" she asked, pointing at the door.

Jack looked at her for a moment and decided on gut feel that she was telling him the truth.

"Yes, they did shoot at me. Okay, let's try this. I'm here to see General Mellig, please," said Jack.

The dark haired woman looked down at a list she had by the phone. She nervously went up and down the list with her finger.

"I..., I don't see a General Mellig, mister. Sorry, we don't get many visitors. You are the first in the four days I've been here," she said.

"Ehhh, I didn't really expect you would find anything, but I thought it was worth a try. What's your name?"

"Margie."

"Margie, do you know what's through that door there?" Jack asked as he pointed at the single wooden door on the long wall that extended the width of the building.

"Uhhh, stuff. I don't know. I've never been in there."

"Margie, I would go home early today. Like right now if I were you. I'm gonna go through that door, and I'm going to destroy most of what's in this building. I don't want you getting hurt. Okay?"

"Destroy? They'll get mad at me if I let you. Probably get fired."

"Maybe, but I don't think so. They will have a lot more to worry about than you."

Jack then walked over to the wooden door. He tried the handle. It was locked, of course. He then made his hand into a fist gave the door knob a gentle punch. The handle broke to pieces. Jack then put two of his fingers into the hole the door knob used to occupy and pulled the door open. A loud alarm immediately started to ring.

Walking inside, the door opened into a mammoth room that appeared to extend the full length of the building. There were five rows of monitor consoles. Each row consisted of monitors fitted back to back, so there were people working on both sides of each row. The people were all wearing the same thing. Grey military style long sleeve shirts, with black pants. Jack's immediate impression was their uniforms actually looked pretty sharp. To Jack's right, there was what looked like a bull pin that the managers of the place appeared to be stationed in. There were seven people seated there.

Everyone in the entire building was staring at Jack. Some standing, but most still sitting. None of them appeared to be working off of an active chip. To the far side of the bull pin area, an elevator door opened, and two of the android robots stepped out with their guns drawn. They immediately began putting rounds on Jack.

For the moment Jack ignored the bullets bouncing off of him. He walked over the bull pin area and made eye contact with a bald man with dark brown glasses. The man was ducking under his desk. Jack peered over the edge of the desk and looked down at him.

"Hey!" Jack said, shouting over the alarm and the gunshots. "Turn off this god damned alarm!"

The man stood up on his knees and hit a few keystrokes on his keyboard and the alarm stopped.

"Now, you guys must have a PA system in here so you can talk to these people. Where is it?"

The bald man stood up on his knees again without saying anything and pointed a few feet away at a PA microphone. Jack walked over and picked it up. He put the microphone to his mouth and pointed at the two androids approaching him. "Enough! Did you not learn from the last time you tried this?"

One of the androids rushed towards Jack and put it's hand on Jack's right shoulder. With his left arm Jack flicked the androids arm off his shoulder. He then quickly reached and placed both his hands on the sides of the machine's head, and raised his right leg kicking the android in the chest. The machine went flying into the far wall, and the impact was so violent it embedded the machine in the wall. Jack was still holding it's head in his hands.

The remaining machine was still firing it's weapon at Jack about fifteen feet away. Jack threw the head in his hands towards the lone remaining android The head struck the machine squarely in it's head, taking it completely off it's body. The machine fell where it stood, and then silence.

Jack bent down and picked up the PA microphone where he had dropped it previously.

"What the hell? Damn it! And, I liked this shirt," said Jack as he was looking down and fingering some of the bullet holes in his shirt.

"Did anyone get hurt?" asked Jack, surveying people around him. All the eyes in the building were riveted on Jack, and not one person acknowledged his question.

"Why am I asking you mother-fuckers? You hurt people every day. Just so you know, I'm here to destroy this place," Jack said as he took in the entirety of the room. It was gigantic.

"You guys know who I am?" asked Jack, as he made eye contact with a woman sitting nearby at one of the consols. She nodded nervously.

"Yeah, I bet you do. I bet you do. This whole chip monitoring, and controlling people's behavior bullshit? It ends today. It ends now.

For christ's sake I gotta be doing you people a favor right? I mean what kind of a shit show job do you have? Talk about soul draining! ...no, this ends today."

Jack quickly glanced back at the bullpen area. All seven people back there were still on their knees. All you could see were their heads peeking over the edge. It was a comical sight to Jack, but he didn't want to get off mission.

"You know my thinking when I came in here was I was going to single-handedly destroy every machine in this place one by one. But, looking at this place, I think that would take the better part of a week."

Jack looked back at the bald guy with glasses. "Does this microphone go over the whole building or just on this floor?"

"It is audible to the entire building" said the guy in glasses, still kneeling behind his desk.

"Okay, here's what's gonna happen. I'm gonna turn this building into a big pile of rubble. It all goes. I'm giving everyone five minutes to get out of the building, and then it comes down. That goes for you people upstairs too. Everyone leaves, or you will probably die." said Jack, into the intercom. A bit of feedback squealed through the speakers, just before Jack removed his finger from the microphone.

And the exodus began. Some ran, there were screams but everyone on the entire floor was moving towards an exit.

Jack felt a tap on the back of his left shoulder.

Turning to look, Jack saw the bald man in the glasses. He could tell right away that he was under the control of someone else.

"You think you can just come in here and destroy my facility and get away with it? Oh no. There will be hell to pay for this."

The bald man pointed at Jack. "You will pay for this, Jack Strong! In the blood of those you care about."

Jack had heard enough. He put his hands on the guys shoulders and turned him around so Jack was facing his back. Then Jack took a hand full of this jacket and just started walking towards the door, dragging the guy along like a suitcase missing a wheel.

When he got to the door, Jack flung the guy down the stairs, and closed the door. He could see the parking lot was filled with people in grey long sleeve shirts and black pants. They weren't dispersing. They were just standing. Anticipating the destruction of the building they were just in. Walking back inside, Jack didn't see anyone. Looking down towards the far end of the long building, he saw no one. Jack was surprised it was that easy to vacate everyone ...now onto the destruction of this building. There were three rows of two-foot diameter cylindrical support poles that ran the entire length of the building. One on either side, and one down the middle. Suddenly Jack could imagine his little brother saying to him "Ram the poles like Juggernaut would."

Jack thought he would start with the far row of columns, and work his way back towards the parking lot side of the building. With a head of steam Jack took the first column out like butter. He didn't know what to expect, but he was surprised how easy it was. In a short time he had run the full length of the building, taking out the entire far row of support columns, and then back again, taking out the entire middle row.

It was working. The entire far side of the building had already collapsed. The middle was still hanging on ...but not for long. Jack started taking out the column nearest to the parking lot. Each time he ran through one of the columns it, made a terrible sound, like a dump truck running over a donut shop.

And when he got towards the end the entire building collapsed on top of him before he could take out the final two columns. Jack felt the weight of the two story building on top of him. He just lay there until all the noise stopped, and the rubble settled.

For the first time since the day his family was killed, Jack felt as though he had actually accomplished something. That he had finally struck a blow back against the generals machine. Not just for him and his family, but for all families affected by this madman.

When all the noise had stopped, Jack pushed enough cement and machines off him to sit up. And, then stand up. What he saw was impressive. A giant mound of cement and metal as long as a city block. *No one would be monitoring the chips anymore,* he thought.

Jack made his way just outside the giant pile of debris. He instinctively reached down to dust himself off, even though his clothes were for all intents in shreds. Then he paused. He could hear something... singing, it sounded like.

We fight our country's battles
In the air, on land, and sea;
First to fight for right and freedom

Jack looked up. All of the black panted workers that were in the building were holding hands singing the Marine hymn. He started walking on a line towards them. As he approached, he muttered under his breath, "Fucking weirdoes."

He stopped about fifteen feet in front of them. He wondered what kind of mind meld the general had them under that they would be singing songs in front of the wreckage of their former building. He looked at them for a brief moment. Most of them stopped singing. All were fixated on Jack. Then, turning and looking towards the parking garage across the street, Jack bent down and fired himself into the air. All the general's employees stood still and watched as Jack followed his long high arc to the top of the parking garage where he had left the heavy cargo van.

"Holly crap! That was freaking biblical!" said Steve, as he was still surveying the damage to the building from the top of the parking garage.

Jack looked around. "Where did the black suit guy go?" he asked.

"He picked up his finger and ran for the stairs right after you jumped down," Karen said. She gave Jack a long once over. "Your clothes are in shreds ...what took ya so long?"

Jack smiled. "Well, I had to get everyone out of the building."

"How will we know if that did it? How will we know if they are no longer able to control people," asked Jack's grandfather.

Jack walked over to Karen, and took the signal blocking device out of her ponytail. "If Karen suddenly goes into zombie mode, we will be the first to know."

Karen put her arms out and began to walk as if she were mummified, and then looked back at Jack with a gigantic smile. A bolt of attraction for Karen warmed Jack's heart. *He was so lucky to have her,* he thought to himself.

Chapter 22

"Are you the one they call Density?" asked a blond girl who looked to be in her early twenties. Her friend, a tall brunette, stood next to her for moral support, both giggling. Both were dressed casually in shorts and a t-shirt.

"Yes, that's me," said Jack, standing next to the edge of a bar about to dig into a hamburger and fries.

"We think you are awesome! You should be a superhero!"

"Thanks girls. Hey if you don't mind, it's been a long day for me and I just want to eat this, okay?" said Jack.

The girls looked at each other and giggled again. "No problem!" said the blonde.

"You're hot!" the brunette said as the girls walked away giggling.

Karen raised an eyebrow, looked at Jack, and giggled.

"In retrospect, I should have worn a lone ranger mask or some kind of disguise at that Bears game," said Jack as he stuffed a fry into his mouth.

The four of them were at a BJ's restaurant. However, they were at the bar because Jack couldn't sit down. Karen sat closest to Jack, followed by Steve, and Jack's grandfather sat farthest away. Jack stood at a corner of the bar so he could see all three of them while they were eating.

"I could have warned you to wear a mask if you had shared your plan of moonshotting onto the field of play during a game," said Steve sarcastically.

"Can you guys believe this crap is finally over? I mean, think about it! No more having to worry about zombie mode. No more

Mellig controlling the globe! Look at these people. They have no idea what we saved them from." said Jack.

Karen looked at Jack's grandpa and Steve, and then back to Jack.

"What if it's not over? I mean, how do we know it's over?" asked Karen sheepishly.

Jack's grandfather spoke up. "You can say what you want about Mellig, but he's not stupid. I just can't see him putting all his eggs into one basket. To be honest with you I'm a little nervous about being in a public place."

Jack took a big sip of his beer and sat it down. "Look at us. Look at where we are. We are at a bar in a restaurant ...in public. Do you see anyone in zombie mode in here? You know there's people in this bar with a chip. But, none of them are being controlled ...because we destroyed the control center."

Jack motioned towards Karen. "Karen has behaved normally since we took the blocker out of her hair clip. She hasn't stabbed her hand again, or anyone else for that matter."

"I really think we are safe," said Steve. "I mean we destroyed the monitoring station. We struck a bigtime blow. Go team Density!"

"You hear that?" said Jack. He could hear whispering. Then, he looked around.

Jack noticed that fully three-quarters of the packed restaurant had their heads facing down towards their plates, and all of them were whispering something. Then, to his horror, he looked and noticed that Karen also had her head facing downward towards her plate. He couldn't see her eyes, but he could hear her whispering too.

Jack's eyes met with his grandfather and Steve. At that moment, they all knew they hadn't won anything. Mellig's menace was as strong as ever.

Jack quickly grabbed the disk next to Karen's plate and inserted it back into her ponytail. Her head quickly rose, and she looked confused. Then she realized what had just happened, and what was happening all around them.

"Oh my god. Oh my god." Steve said, horrified. "We didn't win. I'm pretty sure all we did was piss him off."

Then Jack heard an evil, deep laugh. "Did you really think you could beat me?" the bartender said, standing in front of Jack with the crazy glassy-eyed stare.

"I have dozens of monitoring stations all over the world. You will never! Ever! Stop what's happening. There's absolutely nothing you can do about it."

"I have to tell you I haven't been able to contain my laughter sitting here listening to you four. You really thought you had saved the world!" said the bartender with a maniacal laugh. "The only one that will save the world is me!"

"Right before you tore down my Fort Worth facility, I told you something. Do you remember what that was, boy?"

Jack was drawing a blank. He must have meant when he was talking through the bald guy Jack thought.

"I told you that you would pay for this with the blood of those you care about and love ...and so you will."

The bartender raised a pistol and pointed at Jack's grandpa. The gun exploded into his chest, knocking James off his stool and onto the floor.

Steve got up and started to run for the door. The bartender pointed the gun at him, and discharged a round. He missed. The round splintered a wooden rail near the front door. At a frantic pace, Steve made it to and through the door.

Then the bartender pointed the gun directly at Karen's face. At the last second Jack shoved his hand in front of the barrell. The gun fired and the bullet went into Jack's hand. Jack quickly grabbed the gun and bent the barrel upwards ninety degrees. Without delay he picked Karen up and ran towards the door.

Jack had a pretty good idea his grandpa was dead. He took a shot directly into his heart. At least he saw Steve get out. The thing that tore Jack up was that he couldn't stop and check on his Grandpa yet. He just couldn't. He had to get Karen out. He had to keep her alive no matter what. He couldn't lose all three of them.

Clearing the front door Jack was sprinting towards the cargo van. He held Karen close. One arm under her back and another under her knees. People that were in the parking lot stood still and were staring at Jack. Some of them under the chips control, and some not. He helped Karen into the van. Steve was already there. Jack told them to lock the door, and he went back towards the restaurant.

As he approached the door, random people were sprinting through the doorway. Some screaming, others clearly in a state of shock. Jack walked through the door. The only people left in the restaurant were chipped. They stood silently, stuck on Jack with their wide wide glassy-eyed gazes.

"I just killed your grandpa. I'll get the others too. You're gonna learn, Jack. I'm not one to be trifled with," said the bartender as he rested his elbows on the bar looking down at Jack's grandpa with a sinister grin. Jack bent down and placed his hand on his grandfather's corroded artery, feeling for a pulse. After a moment, he stopped. Looking down at his grandfather's lifeless body, his shoulders slumped a bit, and he covered his eyes with his hand A few seconds later, Jack stood and spoke calmly to the bartender.

"You can hurt others, but you can't hurt me. You signed your death warrant when you had my little brother and my mom killed. Eventually I will find you, and on that day, you will die. And, there is nothing you can do about it."

The bartender stood straight, and there was a very brief wave of fear that flashed across his face. With that, Jack bent down and picked up his grandfather and walked out the door.

After a five minute discussion on what to do with Jack's grandfather's body, the three of them agreed to take his body to the nearest emergency room. That's all they really had time for considering the circumstances. Jack would come back and try to make sure his grandfather's affairs were in order after his friends were safe. After Mellig was dead.

Jack drove for hours. He had to get out of the city Way out of the city. He drove west, in fact they had passed Abeline about an hour ago, and then they took a small road south. They were in the middle of nowhere. He had pulled the cargo van in under a large oak tree at a rest stop. Karen layd prone along one bench in the back. Jack sat on the opposite bench, looking at her.

"Everything we had been planning. Everything we did was all for nothing," Jack said, half angry and half hopeless.

"What's the point, Jack? We can't fight him anymore. He won. We are screwed. The whole world is screwed," retorted Karen, as she moved her fingers through her hair. She'd been crying.

"We're fucked," said Steve, putting his head in his hands while sitting on the bench seat in the truck.

"The only reason I haven't killed myself already is because of this little thing," said Karen, as she showed Jack her ponytail. Displaying the tiny metal piece they had fixed to her scrunchy.

Jack looked at Karen's pony-tail. He was looking at it, but it's like he was staring through it. Staring at something else. He was thinking. And, then his mouth opened a little bit, and his eyes widened.

"What?" Karen asked, studying Jack's face.

"I've got an idea," said Jack, as he stood up and started walking towards the driver's seat.

"But first we need to make three stops," said Jack.

"What stops?"

"Food, gas, and Wal-mart."

Chapter 23

"So, we're clear on what happens next right?" said Jack.

Karen nodded her head. "We stay here with the van."

Steve, sitting on one of the benches in the back stood up and unlocked the back doors and jumped out of the van. "I hope this works, man. This is a big play."

Jack pushed a box with his foot towards the back door of the van. The van creaked and moaned under his massive weight as he took each step.

"Yeah, it's like trying to get checkmate with most of your pieces gone," Jack said.

By this time Karen had exited the van and made her way around the back of the vehicle, standing next to Steve.

Jack, Steve, and Karen spent the better part of two days getting what they needed and driving and, now they had reached their destination. Washington D.C. They were sitting on the top floor of a parking garage off New York Avenue, adjacent to the White House. The top floor of the garage was completely vacant except for their large cargo van.

Jack knew in the back of his mind that Karen and Steve never really believed in his new plan. In spite of that, they supported him, and it seemed to give them a bit of hope and more importantly than anything else, take their minds off the feeling of hopelessness they had both had been mired in from the wake of Jack's grandfather's death.

"How do we know he's even there?" asked Karen.

"I don't know, but I gotta try. Look, they can't hurt me. Let's just see how it goes. But no matter what you guys can't leave this van, okay?" said Jack as he walked to the back of the van and picked up a two foot square cardboard box.

"Mellig is still out there, and he still wants to see you dead," Jack said, as he opened the door to the back of the van.

Jack took the box out of the back of the truck, and set it on the ground next to his feet. Just then Steve started to laugh. Not a normal laugh. Jack knew exactly whose laugh that was. Jack and Karen both looked over at Steve. He had the tell-tale look. Wide, unblinking glassy eyes, and the laugh...

"Steve, cut that out! It's not funny!" Karen said.

Jack continued to study him for a moment. "...Uhh, he's not faking." Quickly Jack took the card out of his pocket and put it behind Steve's head. It turned red, showing Steve had a chip.

"There's no way! I checked him on the bench by the lake in Chicago. He was negative," Jack said.

"Yes, he didn't carry a chip at that time. But, when he left to get his lab equipment, one of my teams picked him up and chipped him. The beautiful part is that he has absolutely no memory of it," said the voice coming out of Steve's mouth, which Jack knew was Mellig.

"No way! He wasn't gone long at all!" Jack said.

Karen raised her hand to Jack, holding out a hat that had been fitted with one of the blocking chips. Jack shook his head at her. He wanted to talk to the bastard Mellig.

"It doesn't take long," laughed Mellig. "Jack, in truth we have been watching you from the moment you left La Marque Texas. The whole way. Your entire journey. I didn't activate Steve's chip until now because I didn't want you aware of it.So, I wasn't necessarily privy to your conversations, but it was worth waiting."

"Why let me destroy your monitoring center if that's true," Jack asked.

"Honestly, I wanted to see if you could do it." said Mellig.

"Then you know why we are here? And, you know what our plans are?" Jack said emphatically.

"I'm not exactly sure what you are up to, but it all ends here. There is no way I can physically stop you from getting into the White House. ...but you can't stop me from killing them all. Do you really want all that blood on your hands Jack?" said Mellig.

"Killing who?" Jack asked.

Steve motioned with his hand towards the guard rail. "Have a gander..."

"What's that noise?" Karen said.

Jack listened. They could hear the faint sound of helicopters. It grew louder and louder, and it seemed like in no time at all there were four Apache helicopters flying in the vicinity of the White House. One of the helicopters moved over close to the top of the parking garage. Jack walked over to the edge of the retaining wall at the top of the parking garage. He looked down to see people pouring out of every building within eye shot. From his perspective atop the parking garage it looked like slow moving ants headed out of these buildings in mass. It struck him the vast extent of Mellig's reach. The unholy stain he had put on all of humanity with his chip program. It was diabolical.

"I will kill them all if you even try to approach the white house ...starting with your two friends here." Steve said with an evil wide grin.

Jack didn't even look back at Steve. He wasn't going to give Mellig the satisfaction. The cement from the guard wall began to crumble under Jack's grip as his anger grew and grew.

"There's no way. There's no way you would kill those people," Jack said. In the back of his mind, Jack was hoping Mellig would point the powerful machine gun on the helicopter somewhere other than at Steve and Karen, which was where it was pointed now.

Steve grinned wide and started to do a fast clap. "You just haven't learned anything, have you? Jack Strong, you don't know me at all! Well, perhaps after this lesson you will learn."

Steve looked at the helicopter near them and nodded his head. The Apache helicopter slowly turned and angled it's nose down at the growing crowd of innocent people that were standing outside the building across the street from the parking garage. That's all Jack was waiting on. Quickly, Jack stepped forward and wrapped his hands around a metal pole with a sign that said *Don't Stand Near The Railing.* It was bolted into the ground. Jack pulled it out of the concrete as easy as pulling a birthday candle out of a cake.. He took one backwards cross step to gain momentum, and flung the pole in the direction of the helicopter. The metal pole sailed on a line directly into the propeller blades of the helicopter. From what Jack could see, at least two of the blades went flying., sending the helicopter spinning downward towards the ground before it shot a single round.

Jack lunged, grabbing the hat from Karen and slapping it on Steve's head

"You two, inside the van and close the doors!" Jack screamed as he pointed at both Karen and Steve.

"What happened?" Steve asked, perplexed.

"Explain to him," said Jack, as he ran back to the edge of the parking garage barrier. He could hear the helicopter near Pennsylvania Avenue start to fire its machine gun into the crowd below. Without giving a second thought Jack started running towards that end of the parking garage that faced Pennsylvania Avenue. When he neared the barrier, he launched himself into the air. Jack had become a pretty good judge of how to jump and get close to his target. He was fixed on the nose of the aircraft when he jumped, but he could tell on his downward approach he was going to miss the nose. He had overshot it. Coming down fast he reached and grabbed the tail of the helicopter. The tail blade came down hard on his shoulder, sending the tail rotor flying into pieces. The helicopter stopped firing its machine gun, and started to spin in a rapid downward spiral towards the ground. Jack could hear alarms sounding inside the aircraft. He knew the pilots were going to die, but there was no other way. If he had to choose between the pilots dying, or the murder of thousands of innocent people, the choice was obvious. Finally, it burst into flames as it crashed into the middle of the street below.

It frightened Jack when the machine burst into flames, because he didn't know how fire would affect him. After all, he was standing right in the middle of it when the explosion happened. He took several steps back until he was out of the circle of flames. Looking down, he vigorously pat down his jeans, which were on fire. Once out, he closely inspected his arms and hands. No burns. *Another new wrinkle,* he thought to himself. *Flame resistant.*

Jack could hear machine gun fire, and he quickly looked up. There were still two Apache helicopters left. The one that was firing was flying over Lafayette Square in front of the White House. It fired down into a crowd of innocent people that were standing near the corner of H Street and 16th Street. It was odd that there were no screams, Jack thought. The people had no control. They were standing there waiting to be murdered by the helicopter fire. He started running towards the White House, and then fired himself into the air. A few seconds later, Jack was standing atop the White House. He had always heard there was a missile defense system on the roof, and sure enough there it was, surrounded by three soldiers watching the Apache helicopter murdering innocent people in the street.

As he approached the missile pod, the soldiers spotted him and began firing their rifles at Jack. He ignored the bullets bouncing off his diamond-hard body. He had bigger fish to fry at the moment. It occurred to him he had no idea how to aim or fire these missiles, but, he could see the ends of the missiles poking out the firing cylinders. Jack leapt onto the top of the missile pod, reached in and pulled out one of the missiles. It was six feet long, and had the diameter of a large coffee cup. Jack picked up the missile and held it atop his shoulder as one would throw a spear. He didn't trust his accuracy from this range. He had to get closer.

Jack jumped again and this time landed in Lafayette Square. The helicopter was just fifty yards in front of him and about one hundred feet high. The moment he landed, the helicopter rotated and began firing it's big fifty-caliber rounds at him. Two rounds hit Jack in the chest. The bullets didn't penetrate his skin, but they hurt. Jack couldn't risk the missile getting hit. He instinctively fired himself into the air on a trajectory that would take him above the rotating blades of the helicopter. The second he was above the helicopter he threw the missle down into the whirling blades. Jack could instantly feel the heat from the massive explosion. He landed close to I street in front of the Veteran's building. Looking back, he could see a boy standing directly under where the inflamed helicopter would land in just seconds. Jack quickly stepped forward. He held out both fists, pointing them directly at the boy and contracted the muscles in his hands and forearms with extreme force. As if pulled by an invisible rope, the boy began to fly through the air on a line towards Jack. Jack caught the boy and immediately turned his back towards the helicopter to shield him from the secondary explosion of the aircraft impacting the ground. Jack couldn't believe it worked. The same way it worked when he used his contracted fists to take the policeman's gun in Missouri. He was able to concentrate the gravitational field.

A surge of anger flooded Jack. He was tired of this bullshit. Placing the kid on the sidewalk, and patting his head, he took off on a dead run towards the final Apache helicopter. It was flying over 17th Avenue near the intersection of Pennsylvania Avenue.

He could hear gunfire coming from it's turret. The helicopter was firing down at a crowd of people in the street

in front of the United Nations Foundation building. All the terrible killing. Jack was becoming numb to it. All it was doing at this point was fueling his drive to take Mellig out. Of course it bothered Jack, but he just couldn't prevent everyone from getting killed by Mellig's machine. He had to stay focused on the mission, and if he could save lives along the way he was going to do it. But there's no way he could stand down like Mellig wanted. No way. Mellig was going to die, and that was the only acceptable outcome. As he neared the helicopter, he launched himself into the air. He hit the bottom of the tail of the aircraft with such force it clipped the tail completely off the helicopter. The fuselage of the craft began spinning wildly and smashed into the parking lot of the Eisenhower office building, bursting into a fireball.

Thirty seconds later, Jack was back on the top floor of the parking garage knocking on the back door of the cargo van. Steve opened the door with a tire iron in his hand ready to strike. He lowered it when he saw it was Jack.

Karen jumped out and hugged Jack. "Thank god you're alright!" she said, kissing him on the cheek.

"Him all right? He can't be hurt. I'm glad we're all right." said Steve, adjusting the cap on his head.

"I took out the helicopters, but there could be more on the way. If we are going to do this we need to do it fast." Jack motioned towards a cardboard box in the cab of the van. Steve picked it up and brought it to Jack.

"Good luck. I wish I could come with you." Steve said.

"You can't. Too dangerous," Jack said emphatically. "Get back in the truck and lock the doors."

Jack took the box and walked to the edge wall of the parking garage. He had studied a map of the White House and knew where the president's office was in the west wing. He couldn't see the front of the White House from where he was, but he knew he wanted to start from the front of it. He took a tight hold of the box, bent down, and shot himself into the air.

It turned out he judged his jump pretty well. He landed on the edge of the Rose Garden to the left of the White House entrance. Jack pulled his feet out of the hole he just created, and double-checked the box. It was intact. *That's good,* Jack thought, *step one accomplished.*

Since the Oval Office was in the west wing, Jack didn't see the point of going through the front door of the White House. So, he headed towards the west colonnade, which was to the left of the front door, to make his way over towards the Oval Office. Jack noticed two armed guards posted towards either end of the colonnade. He was very surprised that they weren't approaching him. They watched him. They noticed him. He could tell they were under the control of the chip ...but they just stood still watching him. Not what Jack expected.

Once he stepped onto the colonnade, he began walking directly towards the door that led into the west wing. The door one of the two soldiers was stationed in front of. Jack locked eyes with the soldier. There was no expression, no emotion, no evil grin. Just a blank stare. Jack couldn't figure it out. This wasn't like Mellig. Jack's experience was Mellig was either aggressive, or he would taunt Jack like the crazy maniacal person he was. As Jack got closer to the door, the soldier stepped aside as if to invite Jack inside. Jack stopped, and studied the soldier. Again, nothing. Then Jack reached and opened the door and stepped inside.

Jack slowly made his way down the hall to the left towards the Oval Office. As he passed an office on the left he saw a woman on the phone. He could tell she was under the control of the chip. She looked at Jack, and placed her hand over the microphone on the phone.

"They are waiting for you in the Oval Office, Jack," she said, and then she took her hand off the lower part of the phone and continued her conversation.

Jack continued, and then arrived at the door to the Oval Office. Opening the door, he walked inside. What Jack saw was otherworldly strange to him. Sitting in two chairs facing each other at an off angle were the President of the United States, and the Prime Minister of Great Britain. There were several others sitting on the nearby couches, and others standing nearby, including the Chief of Staff of the United States, and the majority leader in the Senate. All of them were under the control of the chip. They were silent. Zombied out stare on their faces Jack was all too familiar with. Standing not far behind the President were two guards dressed in black tactical gear with AR-15's shouldered and pointing at the President.

The president looked up at Jack and began to speak.

"Hello, Jack. Interesting move on your part, coming here. Not exactly sure what you are up to, but just in case you try to do anything, these two guards will kill the president."

Jack looked again at the guards. "Understood. So, what exactly is this? They are all under your control. What's the point of them even meeting if you speak for all of them?"

"We have to keep up appearances, Jack ...for those that are not yet under my control. In a moment, we will all go into the Rose Garden for a press conference, where we will say what wonderful and productive talks we just had."

"Ridiculous," piped up Jack.

"You made a mistake coming here Jack. What's in the box? You come bearing gifts?"

"Yeah, you wanna see what's in the box?" asked Jack with a smile on his face.

"I would, yes. Very much so," said the President with a wide-eyed crazy grin.

"Here ya go..." said Jack as he tossed the box on the floor in front of the President. The minute the box hit the floor, Jack pulled a small Glock 43 pistol from his belt. He put a round in each of the legs of the guards, and then another round in their trigger arms. Their guns fell to the ground. Jack quickly ran over and broke each gun in two, and then removed the pistols each guard was carrying and crushed them in his hands.

Jack quickly opened the box. He pulled out a hat and stuck it on the President's head.

"What's going on here? Who are you?" asked the President.

"I'll explain in just a second. Until then, I need you to help put these hats on every man and woman in this room," said Jack, as he plopped a stack of hats on the President's lap.

Jack quickly grabbed another stack and began placing them on the heads of each person in the room. He wasn't sure if the President would actually help him, but sure enough, he was placing hats on heads. In under twenty seconds, every person in the room had a hat on their head. The room suddenly filled with conversation. "What the hell is going?" on was by far the most popular phrase being uttered. Even the guards had a hat on, suffering as they were.

"I'm sorry I had to shoot you guys, but I couldn't have you killing the President. We'll get you medical attention shortly," said Jack.

"I demand to know the meaning of this," said the president.

"How did I get here?" said the Prime Minister.

"Okay, I'll explain, but first I want to show you something," said Jack, as he stepped closer to a woman in the room. Jack wasn't sure who she was, but assumed she was some kind of VIP.

"Madam, if you will permit me, I'm going to remove the hat from your head for just a moment. But before I do that I'm going to give you a word, and when I ask you to repeat the word I'm about to give you, you will simply say that word, okay?"

"I don't think so buddy. Mr. President, we don't even know who this guy is. He walks in here and starts barking orders? To the President of the United States, and the British Prime Minister?" the woman said, her shrill tone raising with each word.

"She does have a point," the President said.

Jack spoke to the collective group. "How did you all get into this room? Do you remember brushing your teeth this morning? What did you do yesterday? When is the last time you saw your spouse?"

The group was silent. They shot quiet, scared glances at each other.

"For most people those are easy questions to answer. I'll explain why you don't know the answers to them, but first let me make this tiny demonstration.

Madam, the test please?"

The woman nodded. "Yes, okay."

"The word is revenge," said Jack. Then he took the hat off her head. Her facial expression immediately changed. Her eyes widened and fixed on the President.

"This is your plan? Hats?" The woman began the crazy laugh of General Mellig.

"What is the word I just gave you?" asked Jack.

"Word? What the hell are you talking about? This will never work, Jack. I will kill them all." the woman said.

Jack quickly placed the hat back on her head. "What is the word I just gave you?" asked Jack.

"Revenge," she said.

"What was that? Why didn't she know the word when the hat was off?" the President asked.

"All right, we don't have alot of time, so I'm gonna try to *Readers Digest* this thing for you. All of you have a chip inserted in the back of your heads that allows others to control what you say and what you do. It's hard to say how long this has been going on, but it's been a while."

"Who inserted these chips?" asked the Prime Minister.

"They were inserted under the direction of a rogue general named Max Mellig. He developed this technology with the idea of taking over the world for all intents and purposes. A task which he has largely completed. I've been trying to fight him myself, but this is too big for me. I need your help."

"Why the hats?" asked the woman that Jack gave the word to.

"Yes, the hats... First, for those of you who aren't Cowboys fans I'm sorry. I bought these in Texas. A good friend of mine, who is the smartest guy I ever met, made a small piece that would block the signal Mellig uses to communicate with the chips. There is one fixed on the back of each of those hats. So, for the first time in a long long time, you are yourselves again. Your thoughts and actions are your own."

"Who are you, and how did you manage to just walk in here?" said the President.

"My name is Jack Strong. I am from La Marque, Texas. I can do things most people can't do, courtesy of General Mellig. A previous project from a long time ago. Anyway, he killed my family, and I've been fighting him ever since. But, to find out where he is and stop this menace I need your help, your assets, your intelligence assets."

For the next ten minutes Jack went into greater detail about how the chips were being spread primarily through medical professionals, and that virtually all important or influential people had been chipped, especially world leaders. He told them about the resistance group that was helping him, and how Mellig had them killed. Then he told them about himself, and how he came to be, and what he could do. How he couldn't be hurt. He told them about the monitoring center in Fort Worth, and how he destroyed it, and how they thought they had won, but they hadn't. He told them about his

Grandpa getting killed. He pretty much told them everything right up until the time he stepped into the Oval Office.

"All of you are in grave danger. I expect Mellig to bring as much muscle as possible into this equation to get those hats off your head, and get things back to the way he wants them. So, here is what I suggest. We need to get you guys into the bunker of this place right now. Then you will tell me the people you need to begin mounting a strategy against Mellig and I will get them. I just need to know where he is, and I need you to help me find him."

"I can get us there now," said the President.

"During the Reagan Administration there was a hidden entrance to the tunnel system and bunker from this office. It's just there." The President pointed to a table against a wall holding a small lamp.

There was a moment of silence after the President's remark, but Jack didn't have time for moments of silence.

"Okay, let's go, let's go! Come on." Jack motioned with his arms for everyone to get up.

"I'm gonna leave you two here. Someone will come to give you assistance," said Jack to the two guards on the ground.

The President got up and moved to the table. He pulled out a drawer on the table, and reached under and inside the drawer to hit a switch of some kind and the entire wall including the table opened up to show a set of stairs. The President went through first, and within thirty seconds they were all descending the long staircase. Jack was last, and pulled the wall together behind him. It struck Jack as a bit comical as he watched about twelve Dallas Cowboys hats trod down the stairs.

Inside the bunker the group joined another group, already working inside the bunker. Actually it wasn't a group. It was two tech guys that happened to be doing some work inside the bunker. Jack saw a need for the tech guys, so he had the group hold back from going into the bunker for a moment. Jack went back up the long staircase and took the hats off the two guys that had been shot, but still laying on the floor.

"Sorry, guys, but I need those hats. You need to call for help. Medical attention. Okay?" said Jack, just before he removed the hats. He took the hats and immediately heard the general and others babbling at him through the soldiers, but he didn't engage. He just headed back down the stairs. Finally, he could get some help in finding Mellig.

Chapter 24

Three weeks later...

General Max Mellig stood behind a brightly-lit kitchen island, cutting up onions on a wooden cutting board. He glanced up briefly to look out the giant wall of glass that was the edge of his living room onto the last glimmer of sun kissing the side of the Arizona mountain behind his home.

Mellig was a tall man, standing every bit of six feet four inches. The caramel-colored apron he had on was not made for such a tall person, covering down to his mid thigh instead of below the knees. He had salt and pepper hair, but the pepper portion of his hair was jet black. There was jazz music playing low in the background. Mellig took a big sip of red wine, and turned to wash his paring knife off in the sink behind him.

Just then, a proximity alarm started going off throughout Mellig's home. Mellig immediately looked up, dried his hands off, and looked at his cell phone. "Proximity alarm!" he said to himself. "Probably coyotes again." At this point, an entire pane of floor to ceiling fifteen-foot glass burst into tiny shards. When Mellig looked up, Jack Strong was standing in his living room.

"Wow, they got it right. You are here. My lucky day!" Jack said.

"What the hell? How did you find me here?" Mellig said in disbelief.

"I had some help from my friends. So, this is where it all happens, huh? Sending out kill orders. Telling the President what to say," said Jack as he walked towards Mellig in the kitchen.

"I don't know who sent you here, but I do know one thing... they would want me alive," said Mellig with a note of panic in his voice.

"Yeah, they did want you alive," said Jack as he inspected a giant spear from what looked like an antique weapons case against the wall adjacent to the kitchen.

"But, you killed my mom and my little brother, so you aren't leaving this house alive, just to be clear," said Jack.

"You would disobey a direct order? From what's got to be the President himself?" Mellig asked.

"When it comes to you? Oh yeah. I'll just have to say, "'oops, I'm sorry'" on that one. And know this: after you're dead, I'm going to throw your body onto that mountain and let the coyotes eat what's left of you," said Jack as he pointed across at the mountain facing them. It thrilled him to be able to say that to Mellig.

Mellig started giggling. "And, then what will you do, Jack? Will you go back to bending metal in La Marque Texas?"

"I don't know. The President offered me a job when this is done," Jack said.

"What kind of job did he offer you?" said Mellig as he laughed.

"I'm the guy they call to get bad guys like you ...and, it came with some perks. They said they would build me a house that I can actually live in without crushing everything, so there's that," said Jack without looking up from examining the spear.

"I knew you would come after me one day, Jack. You didn't think I wouldn't have a weapon ready for you?" said Mellig.

Jack looked up at Mellig, who was pointing what looked like a *Star Trek* phaser at him.

"You see this, Jack? I had this commissioned just for you. It shoots a pulsar blast equivalent to the surface temperature of the sun. It will burn a hole right through you, Jack. So I suggest you turn around and get the fuck out of my house before I end you. Right here! And right now!" said Mellig, as he extended his arm towards Jack.

"Let's see it. I want to see it," said Jack, as he shouldered the spear in his right hand, pointing it at Mellig. He held his left hand away and down and made a fist.

Mellig didn't expect Jack to call his bluff so quickly. He got an angry look on his face and pulled the trigger. The blast was headed directly towards Jacks head ...except the trajectory of the blast changed mid stream and it went directly into Jack's balled up, gravity inducing fist. At the same time Jack let the spear go with the velocity of a rifle shot. The spear struck Mellig squarely in the chest, pinning him to the refrigerator just behind. Mellig's eyes widened. He looked down at the spear and then back at Jack, coughing up blood onto his white granite topped island.

"That was for little Jimmy and my mom," said Jack. He raised his left hand and inspected it, then raised it up for Mellig to see.

"Not even a scratch ...so much for your sun gun. Now, time to feed the coyotes," said Jack, as he approached Mellig.

Standing in front of Mellig, who by this time was mostly dead, Jack pulled the spear from his chest and tossed it onto the floor. He dragged Mellig's body into the living room and dropped the lifeless corpse onto the floor. Jack took out his cell phone and took a picture. Pocketing his cell, he then grabbed Mellig's right arm and right leg with his two hands. He spun around once quickly, and then let Mellig's body fly, smashing through the glass wall of the living room, true to his word, ...Jack threw Mellig all the way to the mountain facing the house. Jack watched as the body hit the side of the mountain, causing a small cloud of dust. He dusted off his hands as if saying to himself, *Mission accomplished.*

Jack stood there in the quiet living room of the monster he just ended. He could hear something. A faint bang, bang, bang. Jack looked around to see if he could isolate the source of the deep low banging sound. It sounded beneath him. He located the stairs and walked down two stories, because the deeper he descended, the louder the sound got. Opening the door at the bottom of the stairs, Jack stepped into a long concrete hallway with a substantial metal door at the end. Jack stood in front of the door. He pulled the thick handle, heard a click, and the heavy door slowly opened.

Standing in front of Jack was a woman that looked to be in her early fifties. She looked tired.

"What's your name?" she asked Jack, with a faint note of recognition on her face.

"My name is Jack. Who are you?"

"My name is Susan. I'm your mother."